EN

'You're a doctor, not a detective,' he said. 'Stick to what you know.

'This is not the sort of place you can wander about vocalising suspicions without some sort of backlash.'

'Is that what you're worried about, Sergeant Ford?' she asked. 'That there's going to be some sort of backlash you can't handle?'

'No,' he said, moving from behind the bench to take her by the upper arms and pull her towards him. 'This is what I'm worried about not being able to handle.' And his mouth swooped down and captured hers beneath the scorching heat of his.

Dear Reader

Like many writers I often get asked where I get the ideas or inspiration for my novels. There are so many ways: magazines, books, television, movies and even music will often trigger a thought. However, it is more often than not the everyday things of life that provide the best inspiration.

About a year ago my husband and I were driving down the Batavia Coast of Western Australia, a beautiful but very isolated stretch of coastline. Out of nowhere a police car appeared and pulled us over. The officer issued my husband with a warning and, while he was polite, he still delivered a rather stern lecture on the dangers of going over the speed limit. While he was speaking I happened to notice a tracheotomy scar on his throat, and it made me wonder if he had been in a high-speed accident in the past.

What better fodder for a novel? A police officer with a tragic past locks horns with a feisty young female doctor on a private mission to the isolated community of Marraburra. Dr Amy Tanner is one of my favourite heroines, and of course the totally gorgeous but brooding Sergeant Ford is a perfect match for her!

Now, I can't guarantee that the next police officer who pulls you over will be as irresistible as Angus, or that the next country GP who treats you will be as dedicated and compassionate as Amy, but one thing I can promise is that there are hundreds of thousands of wonderful professionals just like them, working exceptionally long hours in remote regions just like the fictitious town of Marraburra. I hope that when you read Amy and Angus's story you will spare a thought for them.

With warm wishes

Melanie Milburne

HER MAN
OF HONOUR

BY
MELANIE MILBURNE

MILLS & BOON®
Pure reading pleasure

First published in Great Britain 2007
Large Print edition 2008
Harlequin Mills & Boon Limited,
Eton House, 18-24 Paradise Road,
Richmond, Surrey TW9 1SR

ISBN: 978 0 263 19934 5

Set in Times Roman 16½ on 19 pt.
17-0208-55030

Printed and bound in Great Britain
by Antony Rowe Ltd, Chippenham, Wiltshire

Melanie Milburne says: 'I am married to a surgeon, Steve, and have two gorgeous sons, Paul and Phil. I live in Hobart, Tasmania, where I enjoy an active life as a long-distance runner and a nationally ranked top ten Master's swimmer. I also have a Master's Degree in Education, but my children totally turned me off the idea of teaching! When not running or swimming I write, and when I'm not doing all of the above I'm reading. And if someone could invent a way for me to read during a four-kilometre swim I'd be even happier!'

Recent titles by the same author:

Medical™ Romance
IN HER BOSS'S SPECIAL CARE
A DOCTOR BEYOND COMPARE
  Top-Notch Docs
A SURGEON WORTH WAITING FOR
  24:7
HER PROTECTOR IN ER

Did you know that Melanie also writes for Modern™ Romance? Her stories have her trademark drama and passion, with the added promise of sexy Mediterranean heroes and all the glamour of Modern™ Romance!

Modern™ Romance
WILLINGLY BEDDED, FORCIBLY WEDDED
BOUGHT FOR HER BABY
BEDDED AND WEDDED FOR REVENGE
THE VIRGIN'S PRICE
THE SECRET BABY BARGAIN

To Jennifer and Andrew Ford

And with special thanks
to Sergeant Iain Roy Shepherd,
for his invaluable advice and information
on being a dedicated police officer
both in the city and country.

CHAPTER ONE

IT WAS the screaming siren that annoyed Amy the most. Not to mention the flashing lights, which were totally unnecessary given there wasn't another car in sight and hadn't been for more than an hour on that part of the Western Australian Batavia Coast.

She pulled over to the side of the road and drummed her fingers on the steering-wheel as she watched the officer unfold himself from the police vehicle behind.

He sauntered over with long lazy strides as if he had all the time in the world, which he probably did, she thought with a cynical curl of her lip. He was no doubt below his day's booking quota and had singled her out to nudge it up before he finished his shift.

Amy activated her electric window as he approached and gave him the overly sweet smile that had rarely let her down in the whole twenty-seven years of her life. 'Hi, Officer, was I doing something wrong?' she asked.

'Do you realise what speed you were travelling at, miss?' he asked in a deep voice that contained a heavy dose of reproof.

Hmm, Amy thought. So he's not one to be impressed by a bright white smile. She took off her sunglasses and, using the second weapon in her feminine arsenal, blinked up at him in lash-fluttering innocence with her slate-blue eyes. '*Was* I speeding? I was sure I was well under the limit.'

'I clocked you on my radar doing seventeen kilometres per hour over the legal limit,' he said in the same reproachful tone. 'That's three demerit points and a hefty fine.'

Amy felt a tiny tremor of panic rumble deep inside her. She only had three points left on her licence as it was. If she was to have it revoked out here where there was no public transport worth speaking of, her three-month stint at the isolated medical clinic at Marraburra was going to prove difficult, if not impossible.

OK, this means I will have to rely on weapon number three, she thought as she got out of the car, smoothing down her tight-fitting short denim skirt as she did so.

'May I see your licence?' he asked, still looking at her face and nowhere near her long tanned legs, which produced another twinge of feminine pique inside her.

Amy suppressed a tiny irritated sigh and turning back to her car leaned in and rummaged in her handbag. She dug her licence out from between her stash of credit cards and handed it to him, her fingers coming briefly into contact with his. She felt a sudden jolt of energy pass from his body to hers and snatched her hand back quickly. Jeepers, surely she wasn't getting *that* desperate, she thought with a wry inward grimace. Sure, she hadn't had a man touch her other than a patient since Simon Wyndam had left her more than eighteen months ago, but that didn't mean she had to go all weak at the knees at brushing against a perfect stranger. Although, sneaking a quick glance at him as he examined her licence, she did have to admit he was a rather gorgeous-looking stranger, even if he happened to be a cop.

He was much taller than she had at first

realised, and although he was still wearing his hat she could see he had dark brown hair and olive skin that had clearly seen plenty of sun. The landscape of his face hinted at the man beneath the surface—there was a suggestion of inflexibility in his lean, chiselled jaw and his mouth looked like it rationed its smiles rather sparingly.

'So you're from New South Wales,' he said, removing his sunglasses to meet her eyes.

Amy felt another shock wave go through her when she looked up into the darkest brown eyes she had ever seen. They were fringed with impossibly long sooty eyelashes that partially shielded his gaze from the glare of the late afternoon sun. 'Um…er…yes…' she faltered as her heart did a little flip-flop in her chest.

'Did you drive all the way across the Nullarbor in this?' he asked, giving her cherry-red sports car what could only be described as a scathing glance.

Amy felt her hackles rising. 'No,' she said a little stiffly. 'I had it shipped on the train and drove up here from Perth.'

'Are you aware of the Western Australian maximum speed limit, Miss Tanner?' he asked.

Amy put up her chin. 'It's *Dr* Tanner,' she said with a hint of professional pride.

His top lip lifted slightly in what suspiciously looked like a smirk. 'Well, then, *Dr* Tanner,' he drawled with insulting exactitude, 'I suggest you slow down or you might find yourself without a licence or even worse—without a life.'

'I wasn't speeding,' she bit out, her patience finally running out. 'I had my car set on cruise-control the whole time.'

'Then perhaps you need to have your speedometer recalibrated, Dr Tanner.'

She sent him an icy glare. 'How typical of a cop to blame someone else's equipment when it very well could be yours that's faulty,' she said. 'Have *you* had yours checked to see if it's working as it should?'

His dark eyes gleamed with a spark of sardonic amusement. 'I can assure you, Dr Tanner, there's absolutely nothing wrong with any of my equipment.'

For some inexplicable reason Amy's eyes dipped to his middle where his gun belt was hanging with all its impressive attachments on his lean waist. She felt her cheeks flare with colour and forced her gaze upwards to meet his black-brown eyes.

'Are you going to book me?' she asked, resorting to one last attempt at her eyelash-fluttering routine which had got her out of more tight spots than she could remember.

He appeared to give the matter some thought, his tongue moving inside his cheek as he looked down at her. Amy tried not to squirm under his scrutiny, but as each pulsing second passed she felt as if his eyes were seeing things she would much prefer to keep hidden.

'I'm going to give you a warning this time,' he said at last. 'But you need to remember these are unfamiliar roads to you, with long stretches between towns. You're not only putting your own life at risk but those of others. Medical help is not around the next bend either—it's a four-hour road trip to Geraldton, or a flight with the Royal Flying Doctor Service.'

Amy had to bite back her stinging retort. Who did he think he was, giving her a roadside lecture on road safety awareness? She had done enough trauma training to know the risks. And apart from those few little suburban speeding tickets on her record, which had more to do with revenue-raising by the district police force than lack of care on her part, she was a perfectly capable and safe driver.

'Thank you,' she said, with a measure of forced gratitude. 'I'll try to be more careful in future.'

He put his sunglasses back on. 'Where are you heading to?' he asked.

'Marraburra,' she answered.

'Are you touring or visiting someone?'

'I'm…going there to work,' she said, hoping he hadn't noticed her slight hesitation. 'I'm doing a three-month locum at the medical clinic.'

'So you're filling in for Jacqui Ridley, are you?'

'Yes,' she said. 'She's taken maternity leave.'

A small silence swirled in the hot dusty air for a moment. Amy couldn't help wondering if he was deliberately allowing it to continue to force her to reveal her real reason for taking such an out-of-the-way and short-term post. It was a cop tactic she was well used to, but there was no way she was going to tell him she was here to visit the place where her cousin Lindsay had recently committed suicide.

'Jacqui's husband is one of the other police

officers in town,' he finally said, replacing his sunglasses. 'There are four of us stationed at Marraburra.'

Amy said the first thing that came into her head. 'That seems rather a lot of cops for such a remote area.'

'Maybe, but, then, it seems to me rather a long way to come for just three months,' he countered neatly. 'You'll hardly have time to unpack before you leave again.'

Amy wondered what motivation was lurking behind the casually delivered comment. There was something about the cop's demeanour that, in spite of the dark impenetrable screen of his sunglasses, suggested he was watching her closely. But, then, she reminded herself, a lot of cops saw everyone as a potential criminal—he was probably no different.

'Perhaps, but I've not long come back from England,' she said. 'I was at a loose end so I thought I'd take this post until I decide what I want to do.'

'Seems reasonable,' he said, but Amy couldn't help feeling his tone suggested he thought otherwise.

'Well,' she said, stretching her mouth into a tight smile. 'I'd better let you get back to what you're supposed to be doing.'

'This is what I'm supposed to be doing,' he said. 'But I'm just about to knock off.'

'So I was the last hope of the day, was I?' she asked, and then added before she could stop herself, 'One last ticket to impress the boss.'

'Actually,' he said, removing his sunglasses once more to meet her up-tilted gaze, 'I *am* the boss. The only person I have to impress out here is me.'

Amy felt the wind taken right out of her self-righteous sails. He didn't look old enough to be the senior officer in town—he was maybe thirty-three or -four, according to her rough reckoning. But then she saw the stripes on his shirt which indicated he held the rank of sergeant.

A man in his reproductive prime. Her mother's voice echoed in her ears. She hastily shoved the thought aside. Her mother was desperate for grandchildren. Whenever she could, she purposely wound up Amy's biological clock. Not that Amy needed any help in that department; she could feel it ticking like a time bomb herself every time she thought of her ex-boyfriend Simon and his new wife and baby son.

'Well, no doubt I'll see you around some time,' she said, affecting an airy tone.

'No doubt.'

She shifted from foot to foot and gave him another on-off smile. 'Er... Could I have my licence back?' she asked.

He handed it to her, his fingers meeting hers again. 'It's not such a great photo,' he said indicating the wide-eyed mug shot on her licence.

Amy wasn't sure what to make of his comment. She hadn't thought it *that* bad. She'd had her chestnut hair specially highlighted and had even put on some make-up, but she had to admit the prior weekend on call had probably taken its toll regardless. She stuffed it back in her purse without responding and got back behind the wheel.

'Take care when driving at dusk,' he added. 'The kangaroos are as big as horses out here. If you hit one in a car this size you're going to come off second best.'

'Thank you for the safety lecture, Sergeant,' she said tersely. 'But I do know how to drive. I might have spent the last year overseas but I am well aware of the dangers on Australian roads.'

'The biggest danger out here is excessive speed. Keep an eye on it, Dr Tanner,' he said, and, tapping her car on the roof with his hand, walked back to his car.

Amy watched in her rear-vision mirror as his long legs ate up the short distance, his broad shoulders having to almost hunch together to get back into the car as he slid back behind the wheel.

She was familiar enough with cops, city or country, to know he wouldn't pull out until she did so. She flicked on her indicator and, checking for traffic—she used the term loosely by Sydney and London standards—pulled out and drove at a snail's pace, with him on her heels the whole way into the tiny remote settlement of Marraburra.

The township was even smaller than she had been expecting and in spite of her personal mission she felt her heart begin to sink. It was going to be a long three months. What on earth did people do out here to keep themselves occupied? she wondered as she drove past the small general store, a café-cum fish and chip shop, the rundown-looking hotel with a pub attached where she had booked in to stay, and a single service station. There was a shoebox-sized post office and a tiny pharmacy which was located next to the medical clinic.

She turned into the clinic parking area and watched as the police car continued on, three blocks down the street to where the police station was situated.

The late afternoon heat was fierce as she got out of the car, and she could hardly wait to get into the cool air-conditioned clinic.

A middle-aged woman looked up from the reception desk as Amy came in. 'Can I help you?' she asked.

'Hi. I'm Amy Tanner, the new GP filling in for Dr Ridley. I've just arrived in town,' Amy said with a friendly smile.

'Oh, Dr Tanner—it's so nice to meet you, Amy.' The woman got to her feet and, proffering her hand over the counter, gave her a firm handshake. 'I'm Helen Scott, the receptionist for the clinic. We've been looking forward to you arriving.'

'Thank you,' Amy said. 'It's great to be here at last. It was a long drive.'

Helen gave her a knowing smile. 'It's a long drive to anywhere out here. You get used to it. You've been in London for the past year, Allan Peddington, our other GP, was telling me. This will be a right change from that, I imagine.'

'I'm looking forward to the challenge of working in a remote area,' Amy said. 'And I've never been to Western Australia before so it will be a bit of an adventure.'

'We've organised a little welcome thing for you down at the pub tonight,' Helen said. 'You can meet some of the locals. The hotel's where you're staying, isn't it?'

Amy couldn't help wondering if her plan to stay at the hotel had been the right decision. She had reasoned when she'd booked in that it was only going to be for three months, and while she hadn't been expecting the Ritz, the Dolphin View had looked a lot less attractive as she'd driven past just now than the Marraburra website had portrayed.

'Yes,' she said distantly. 'I thought it would be close to the clinic.'

'Well, it's certainly close to everything, but

that might not be what you want after a hard day's work,' Helen said, confirming Amy's suspicions. 'If it doesn't work out I know someone who has a spare room for rent at his house near the beach at Marraburra Point. He had a boarder move out a couple of weeks ago. It's about a fifteen-minute drive from here but well worth the view. '

'I'll keep that in mind,' Amy said, privately hoping she wouldn't have to resort to sharing a house with a perfect stranger after what had happened to her in London. The all-night parties and constant stream of women trailing in and out to visit her flatmate Dylan Janssen had nearly driven her crazy.

'Allan's been called away on a family matter but he'll see you tonight at the pub with the rest of us, say, about seven?' Helen said.

'Seven. Great,' Amy said, dreaming of lying flat in bed after her long drive. 'Do you mind if I have a quick look around the clinic? So I'm a bit more prepared.'

'Sure,' Helen said, and got to her feet with a smile. 'But there's not a lot to see. It won't take long.'

Amy followed the older woman as she showed her through the small two-doctor practice. Apart from basic resuscitation equipment, portable X-ray machine and the standard equipment trolley with its array of bandages and dressings, and one bed for stabilising patients prior to transfer, there was nothing in the way of the high-tech medical gear she'd grown used to working with in a large teaching hospital. But then she reminded herself she wasn't here to further her career. She was here to find out what had led her cousin to take her own life.

'Allan will explain the details about patient transfer to you tomorrow,' Helen said. 'But as you've already seen, this is a remote area. We have a volunteer ambulance, the guys are trained to St John's Ambulance standard. A paramedic ambulance has to come up from Geraldton, or we have to call in the Flying Doctor Service.'

'I understand,' Amy said. 'So what about nursing support? How many do you have attached to the clinic?'

'Well, we only have two nurses at the moment,' she said. 'We could do with more but it's hard to fill country posts nowadays—no one wants to give up the high life in the city.'

Amy knew all about the difficulty of attracting good staff to isolated areas. The long hours and lack of back-up always took their toll in the end. She had even toyed with the idea herself, quite fancying the idea of getting to know one's patients more intimately than the time constraints of working in a large busy city practice allowed, but she knew her mother would have a blue fit if she lived so far away. As it was, Grace Tanner had flown to London three times in the year Amy had spent there.

'What about community support for the elderly or mentally ill?' she asked.

A shadow passed briefly over the older woman's features. 'We do what we can but it's pretty ad hoc,' she admitted, returning to her chair behind the counter. 'If people don't ask for help it's hard to give it to them.' She paused for a moment before adding, 'We had a suicide a few months back. In a community as small as this, everyone feels guilty.'

'Who committed suicide?' Amy asked, hoping she sounded just casually interested.

Helen's sun-lined forehead became even more furrowed. 'A woman in her early thirties,' she said. 'She was an artist, not a professional one—she sort of just dabbled, if you know what I mean. She was a bit of a loner, kept to herself most of the time. She lived in a tiny shack out near the dunes at Caveside Cove a bit further round from Marraburra Point.'

'Was there any indication she was contemplating ending her life?' Amy asked.

Helen's grey gaze flickered again with the shadow Amy had seen earlier. 'I don't usually talk about this but my younger brother committed suicide when he was nineteen,' she said. 'It was such a shock. No one suspected a thing. He'd broken up with his girlfriend but no one thought it would cause him to take his life. In Lindsay Redgrove's case, however, at least there was a history of depression and mental illness.'

'I'm so sorry about your brother,' Amy said gently, thinking of what her uncle and aunt had gone through. 'It must have been truly devastating for you and your parents.'

'They never got over it,' Helen said with haunting sadness. 'None of us have really, even after all these years. That's why I feel so damned guilty about Lindsay. I can't help feeling I could have done something to stop her. There are a few of us around here who feel like that.'

'Was she close to anyone in particular?' Amy asked.

'One or two of the locals got to know her a bit,' Helen said. 'And I always stopped to chat to her whenever she came into town or the clinic. But as I said, she pretty much kept to herself. She didn't make friends easily. I think it had something to do with her background. I heard she'd been institutionalised when she was younger. She didn't trust people much.'

Amy was cautious about asking too many pertinent questions. 'So she was pretty eccentric, then?'

'Yes, she was a quirky sort of person—childlike in a sort of a way, innocent and a bit naïve at times. Some people around here thought she was mad. But from what I saw, as long as she took her medication she was fine.'

Even though Amy knew the circumstances of her cousin's death she thought it was appropriate to continue her line of questioning. 'How did she take her life?'

'An overdose of the medication she was on.'

'Did she leave a note?'

'No, but the coroner's report along with the investigating officer's said the same—it was suicide, nothing more…' Helen said.

Amy frowned at the receptionist's left-hanging-in-the-air tone. 'But you have some reservations about that verdict?' she asked.

Helen gave her a smile touched with sadness. 'When my brother took his life so suddenly and unexpectedly I was determined someone must have done it, you know—murdered him. He didn't leave a note either. But Lindsay's parents seemed resigned to the fact that at some stage she was going to end it all. Apparently she'd tried a few times in her teens before she was diagnosed with a mental disorder, and a couple of times afterwards. I can't help thinking they felt it was almost a relief to put it all behind them. They came and took some of her paintings and a few personal belongings but her shack is still out there, as if she's going to walk back in any minute.' She gave a little shudder and added, 'I took a small wreath I'd made out there just after she died but the place gave me the creeps the whole time I was there.'

'Why is that?' Amy asked.

Helen gave her upper arms a rub with her hands, as if warding off a chill. 'It's never been a particularly popular beach—too far from any conveniences—and to make it worse a couple of teenagers were killed about twenty years ago when a rockfall occurred in one of the caves they were camping in. The surf out there is rough and there's usually a big undertow, so the locals more or less keep to the main beach at Marraburra.' She gave Amy a sheepish look and confessed, 'I know this is going to sound really dumb but a lot of people around here think the place is haunted. I don't know why Lindsay wanted to live way out there in the first place. I certainly wouldn't.'

'Perhaps she enjoyed the solitude. A lot of creative types enjoy being alone to reflect on their work,' Amy said.

Helen smiled. 'You know, it's a real shame you didn't come here when Lindsay Redgrove was still alive. I have the feeling you would have got on with her famously. You seem to have the right attitude to mental illness. Let me tell you a lot of people around here aren't as understanding.'

Amy hoped her guilt at not revealing her true

connection to Lindsay wasn't showing on her face. 'Thank you,' she said, and added wryly, 'I'm glad *you* think so.'

Helen's brows rose slightly. 'Have you had trouble with someone already?'

'I was pulled over by a cop coming in to town,' she said. 'I was bang on the speed limit but he wouldn't listen. Told me my speedometer was faulty.'

'Did he give you a ticket?'

'No, he gave me a warning and a bit of a lecture.'

Helen's expression softened. 'That would be Sergeant Ford. You should consider yourself lucky. He's got a real thing about speeding, but he's all right when you get to know him.'

'I'm not planning on getting to know him,' Amy said determinedly. 'My father was a cop. He made my mother's and my life hell until he left when I was nine.'

'I suppose there are good and bad cops just like there are good and bad doctors,' Helen offered.

'I guess you're right,' Amy said, suddenly regretting her uncharacteristic disclosure. She hardly ever spoke of her father to anyone. She hadn't seen him in years—the last she'd heard he'd left the force and was living in an alcoholic haze with his fourth wife.

'You'd better go and check in at the hotel,' Helen said. 'Don't dress up for tonight. Everyone's pretty casual around here, even the cops.'

Yeah, right, Amy thought cynically as the dark, serious features of the highway patrol officer came to mind when she glanced down at the police station on her way out to her car. She felt like driving past, putting her foot down and doing a burn-out just to annoy him, but there was no sign of him or his car.

CHAPTER TWO

THE pub was stuffy and crowded and smelt of beer and perspiration as Amy walked in to check into her room. Every head swivelled to look at her, the sudden silence making her feel like a piece of meat in a piranha tank—every eye was assessing her and she couldn't help noticing that every one of them was male.

The bartender gave the bar a quick wipe with a cloth as he directed a roving eye over her chest before meeting her eyes. 'So you must be the new doctor.'

'Yes,' Amy said, amazed at the speed of the town's grapevine. 'Amy Tanner.'

'Bill Huxley,' he said and stretched out a massive paw of a hand to grip hers. 'Your room's ready upstairs, number three. I'll get the key for you.'

Amy surreptitiously massaged her crushed fingers as he lumbered away for the key.

'I wonder if there's anyone who could help me upstairs with my things?' she asked as he returned and handed the key over the bar.

A snicker of laughter came from behind her and a slurred voice called out. 'There aren't any bell boys here, girlie. But buy me a drink and I'll ashist you to your room.'

Amy turned to see a man in his mid to late forties leering at her, a beer in one hand and several more empty ones on the table where he was sitting. She drew in a tight breath and sent him a polite smile. 'Thanks for the offer,' she said, 'but actually I think I can manage.'

'Put a lid on it, Carl,' Bill Huxley said, and addressing Amy added, 'Don't mind him, he's had one too many like the rest of them in here. I'll get your stuff up to your room as soon as I can.'

'Thank you, Bill,' she said and made her way to the rickety staircase which led to the upper floor. She came to the door with a number three hanging lopsidedly on it, and as she opened it she was surprised the window on the opposite wall wasn't broken by the doorknob, the space inside was so limited. The room itself looked clean enough. The narrow single bed was made up with a faded orange chenille bedspread which made her think longingly of her queen-size orthopaedic-approved mattress, fluffy down pillows and superfine Egyptian cotton quilt and sheet set on the other side of the continent.

The floorboards creaked noisily as she took the two steps across to the small window, the heat from the afternoon sun hitting her in the face like a slap as she pulled the worn curtains aside. She fanned her burning face with her hands and blew out a breath, her shoulders sagging as the three months stretching ahead of her suddenly became even more daunting.

She turned and out of the corner of her eye saw a dark black shape scuttle across the floor and disappear beneath the bed. Fear clogged her throat and her heart began to hammer erratically as she imagined those eight hairy legs making a pathway across her pillow some time during the night. She forced herself to breathe through her panic, taking deep controlled breaths that were supposed to help her confront and deal with her phobia, as the very expensive cognitive behaviour therapist she had seen in London had promised.

There was a knock at the door and she edged

her way along the wall well away from the bed to answer it, her eyes going wide when she saw the police officer she'd met earlier standing there with her luggage in his hands.

'Oh…' she said, flushing furiously.

'Bill asked me to bring these up,' he said. 'Where do you want them?'

'Um…' She stepped back to let him in and said hesitantly, 'Anywhere's…er…fine.'

He placed her two bulging suitcases and doctor's bag on the floor next to the bed and straightened. Suddenly the room seemed a whole lot smaller, and not just because of her oversized luggage. It felt as if someone had sucked most of the air out of the room, leaving only a tiny ration that made her feel as if every breath she took in was somehow connected to him.

He was out of uniform now, dressed in jeans and a close-fitting white T-shirt that showed off his toned body to perfection. In fact, he had muscles in places she hadn't even seen in *Grant's Atlas of Anatomy.*

'I'm Angus, by the way,' he said, offering her his hand. 'Angus Ford.'

Amy slipped her hand into the dry solid

warmth of his, the brush of his slightly calloused fingers sending a current of electricity through her all over again.

'How are you settling in?' he asked, releasing her hand.

'Um…fine…' she said, trying not to glance past him nervously.

He gave the room a sweeping glance before returning his eyes to hers. 'It can get quite noisy here. If you can't handle it let me know and I'll organise alternative accommodation. I have a spare room for rent at my place if you're interested.'

So *he* was the one with the spare room. Spiders or no spiders, there was no way she going to share a house with him! He'd probably book her for sleeping in or leaving a cup unwashed or something.

'I'm sure this will be perfectly fine,' she said with a tiny hitch of her chin.

He held her look for a little longer than was necessary. 'I suggest you lock your door at night,' he said. 'The natives can get a little restless out there.'

'I'm a big girl, Sergeant Ford,' she said, straightening her shoulders. 'I can look after myself.'

It was absolutely typical, Amy thought, that

that wretched spider chose exactly that moment to make its next curtain call. She watched in frozen horror as it made its way up the curtain from behind her bed. Even though she desperately tried to contain her reaction, her legs began shaking and her palms became sticky from the rush of adrenalin flooding her system.

'Is everything all right?' Angus asked, frowning at her expression.

'Er...' Amy began to flap her hands in panic, her months of therapy completely obliterated when the spider paused on the wall as if deciding which direction to take next. 'Th-there's a big hairy spider behind you... *Oh, no!*' she screeched as it dropped from the wall to land in a grotesque configuration on her pillow. 'Get it off! *Get it off!* Oh, my God, get that thing out of here!'

Angus calmly picked up the pillow and carried it to the window where he released the spider before turning back to face her with an amused expression on his darkly handsome face.

Amy glared at him before he could speak. 'Don't you dare, *dare* laugh at me,' she said through tight lips.

His lips twitched but didn't make the full

distance into a smile. They didn't need to, she noted with resentment. His dark brown eyes were more than doing the job for them.

'Don't tell me a big girl like you is scared of a tiny spider,' he said with a faint trace of mockery in his tone.

'All right, I won't tell you,' she responded tartly. 'And it wasn't tiny—it was huge.'

'It was completely harmless,' he said. 'We get them all the time during the dry season.'

Amy gave a visible shiver and hated that he saw it. 'I don't care what season they like, as long as they stay out of my room and out of my bed,' she said.

'My offer of a room still stands if you find the company here a little offputting.'

'Thanks but, no, thanks,' she said, pleased that her terse response had hit the mark. She saw the way his eyes hardened slightly as if he wasn't used to having women say no to him, and privately congratulated herself.

But as if to test her resolve a ruckus suddenly erupted downstairs, the shouts and swearing and overturned chairs echoing like thunder through the floorboards.

Angus stepped towards the door. 'I'd better sort this out. Let me know if you change your mind.'

'I won't be changing my—' she said, but he'd already gone.

Amy winced as she heard another chair hit the floor and then listened as Angus's deep authoritative voice sounded out. 'Come on, Carl, give it a break. Time to go home, mate, and sleep it off.'

'You can flaming well go to hell,' she heard Carl shout, throwing in a few choice expletives for good measure. 'I want another drink now!'

There was the sound of another scuffle and a glass breaking, as well as a few grunts as a punch or two landed on someone.

Amy couldn't stop herself from rushing from her room to see if help was needed. She raced downstairs to see Angus Ford restraining Carl with one hand, the muscles of his arm bulging as he led him to the door by the scruff of the neck. Angus's other hand was dabbing a handkerchief at his left eyebrow, which was bleeding profusely.

'You'd better get the doc here to see to that eye of yours, Sarge,' Bill said as he tried to right what was left of one of the chairs.

'I'll be fine,' Angus ground out, and tightened his hold on the struggling Carl.

Amy watched helplessly as Angus hauled the drunken man outside, bundling him down the street towards the police station.

'He won't even remember that tomorrow,' Bill said, coming to stand next to her in the doorway.

She turned to look at him. 'Carl, you mean?'

He nodded grimly. 'He shouldn't drink on the medication he's on, but what can you do? He lost his wife and two little daughters in a road accident a couple of years back. He drinks to forget.'

'How terribly sad,' she said. 'What medication is he on?'

Bill's lip curled. 'Antidepressant of some kind. Waste of money if you ask me. Nothing's going to bring Julie and his little girls back. Nothing.'

Amy frowned as she looked at the two men in the distance—Angus tall and in control, and the broken, stumbling, drunken man beside him. She'd had no idea such a small town could contain such drama and sadness.

'You'd better go down and see to Angus's eye,' Bill said. 'Allan Peddington won't be back from Geraldton yet. Looks to me like it needs stitching up.'

Amy frowned as the hotel owner went back inside. Then, blowing out a little sigh, she went upstairs to collect her doctor's bag, came back down and walked the short distance to the police station.

The police station was actually a small house which had been modified to serve its new purpose. On a pole by the front gate was a white sign with POLICE painted in blue letters on both sides. It looked as if someone had used it for target practice as it was pockmarked with four or five rusty bullet holes. The front verandah had been filled in, and there were metal grilles on the windows. Amy opened the front door, and entered the front office, which was adorned with the usual array of missing-person posters and police notices pinned to corkboards on the walls, and a tall counter, behind which sat Angus Ford, pressing his now bloodstained handkerchief to his eye. From somewhere in the rear of the house emanated muffled bursts of slurred expletives interspersed with the occasional sob.

He looked up as she approached the front desk, his dark brown gaze containing a hint of annoyance. 'What can I do for you, Dr Tanner?' he asked as he got to his feet. 'Or have you changed your mind about my offer?'

'No,' Amy said. 'I'm here because that eye looks like it needs medical attention.'

'I'll see Allan Peddington when he gets back from out of town,' he said, and turned back to the papers on the desk.

Amy stood in a seething silence. How dared he dismiss her as if she were a schoolgirl?

'Do you have something against female doctors or is it just women in general?' she asked with a glittering look.

His head came up and his gaze pinned hers. 'On the extremely rare occasions when I have been unwell, or in need of medical attention, I have been Allan Peddington's patient. I see no point in switching now, irrespective of your sex or your skill.'

'Dr Peddington is not present and in my expert medical opinion you need to have at least two or three stitches in that cut, and soon, otherwise it will leave a nasty scar if the edges aren't pulled together properly,' she informed him in her best stern doctor's voice.

There was another brittle silence; even the noise from Carl in the lock-up out back had stopped.

'Will you at least let me take a closer look at it?' she asked.

She heard the slow release of his breath as he moved across to open the waist-high barrier that separated the office from the front. 'All right,' he said. 'But make it snappy. I've got to run Carl home once he cools down.'

'Is there anywhere you can lie down?' Amy asked.

'Not unless I bunk down with Carl, so whatever you have to do, do it here,' he said with increasing impatience as he rolled his chair back and sat down.

Amy opened her doctor's bag, took out a sterile pad and applied it to quell the trickle of blood running down his face.

'Sorry if this hurts,' she said, annoyed that her voice sounded scratchy instead of in control and doctor-like. She suddenly realised she was practically standing between his open thighs, their hard muscular presence so close she felt a tiny flicker of nervousness, or was it excitement?

Don't be stupid, she remonstrated with herself. He's a cop, remember? You don't do cops or control freaks and he's both.

She checked the bleeding after a moment, trying not to notice the citrus grace notes of his aftershave as they drifted towards her nostrils. 'It needs three stitches,' she said. Looking down at his blood-spattered T-shirt, she added, 'Perhaps you'd better take your T-shirt off. Have you got something else you can put on?'

'I've got a police shirt in the cupboard out back,' he said as he hauled his T-shirt over his head and tossed it to one side.

Amy had trouble keeping her eyes from widening as she took in his pectoralis majors and his six-pack of rectus abdominus muscles, deciding she would never be able to look at *Grant's Atlas* in quite the same way again.

She distracted herself by concentrating on drawing up 10 ml of 1 per cent xylocaine with ad-renalin. 'This is going to sting for a minute,' she warned him, and injected the local anaesthetic into the edges of the wound after swabbing it with antiseptic. But unlike every other patient into whom she had injected local anaesthetic, Sergeant Angus Ford didn't even flinch.

She opened a small suture pack from her bag and onto it opened a 4/0 nylon, some sterile gauze squares and a squirt of cetrimide, then donned a pair of sterile gloves. After swabbing the wound and putting a couple of gauze squares onto his eye to soak up the diminishing trickle of blood, she inserted three sutures, bringing the edges of the cut together and stopping the bleeding.

'There,' she said. 'That's better. I'll put a sticking plaster on it now and you can change it each day. I'll need to remove the sutures in five or six days. Are you up to date with your tetanus cover, do you know?'

'Yes.' Then after a small pause he added, 'Thanks. You can send me the bill.'

She shifted her eyes from the dark brown intensity of his. 'There's no charge,' she said as she stripped off her gloves and began clearing away the mess.

'I wonder if I had booked you, as I intended doing, would you have said the same?' he mused as he got to his feet. 'Or perhaps I redeemed myself by removing your eight-legged roommate.'

She turned back to face him. 'It's not too late to slap a speeding fine on me if that's what you want to do, Sergeant Ford. Is that how you get your kicks out here? Charging innocent people with made-up offences to pass the time?'

The slight, almost undetectable tightening of his mouth was the only clue that he was irritated by her jibe. 'How many road accidents have you attended, Dr Tanner?' he asked.

Amy disguised a small swallow. 'Not many…'

'How many?'

'Er…none…' She felt her face grow hot.

'You city doctors are all the same,' he bit out, this time not bothering to conceal his anger. 'By the time the casualties get to you they've been patched up by the ambos or concealed in a body bag. You don't have a clue what it's like to be the first on the scene, identifying bodies, some of them your own friends, locating body parts and who knows what else. You need to think about *that* the next time you get behind the wheel of your fancy little high-performance sports car, *Dr* Tanner.'

Amy stood her ground but only as a matter of

personal pride. She knew her experience at the coal face was limited; she had done the Early Management of Severe Trauma course and passed it easily, admittedly with mock-up patients and scenarios, but that didn't mean she wouldn't be able to handle a real-life emergency and she resented him for implying it.

'You really do have a problem with women, don't you, Sergeant?' she said. 'Tell me something, are you married?'

His dark brows snapped together. 'What sort of question is that?'

'If you are, I pity your wife,' she said. 'I bet you'd slap a ticket on her for smiling without your permission. I've met cops like you before— total control freaks who like to push their weight around just for the heck of it.'

'I'm not married,' he said. 'Not that it's any of your business. But while we're on the subject of personal questions, I've got a couple of my own.'

She drew herself up to her full height but he still seemed to tower over her. 'Go on, fire away,' she said.

'What brings a young woman out into the middle of nowhere for only three months?'

'I told you—I'm doing the locum for Jacqui Ridley.'

'And after that?'

'I haven't decided.'

'So there's no boyfriend or husband to go back home to?' he asked.

'No.' As soon as Amy had said it she wished she hadn't. It made her sound desperate and dateless, a woman rapidly approaching thirty with no man in her life.

'This is a rough place, Dr Tanner,' he said. 'It might not look like it on the surface but let me tell you it's not a picnic out here. If you think the spiders are terrifying, wait until you meet some of the locals.'

'Then why are you here?' she asked. 'What made you come to such a dead-end place?'

A shutter seemed to come down over his face. 'It suits me for now,' he answered.

'Well, this suits me for now, too,' she retorted. 'Now, if you'll excuse me, I have to get ready for the town's welcome for me tonight.' She gave him an arch look, and added, 'I don't suppose you'll be coming?'

'I already have something else planned.'

'Fine, then,' she said, surprised at the little nick of disappointment that pierced her. She picked up her bag and, brushing past him, left before she was tempted to ask him what he had planned. It was none of her business. She didn't want to know.

Well…perhaps only a tiny *weeny* bit…

CHAPTER THREE

HELEN was the first to greet Amy as she came downstairs on the dot of seven. 'I'm sorry to tell you that Allan Peddington can't make it,' she said. 'He's been held up in Geraldton. His daughter lives there and she's had some sort of personal crisis. Boyfriend issues, I think.'

'That's OK,' Amy said with a rueful grimace. 'Believe me, I know all about that sort of thing.'

'Come over and meet the rest of the gang,' Helen said, and led her to a cluster of tables. 'Everybody, this is Amy Tanner, the temporary GP filling in for Jacqui.'

'Hi, Amy.' A woman of a similar age to Helen extended her hand. 'I'm Teresa Clarke, one of the nurses, and this is Kathy Leeman, the other one.'

The introductions were made, although Amy had trouble remembering all their names. But in the end it didn't matter as everyone seemed intent on having a few drinks and kicking back to relax from a hot summer's day.

After a couple of glasses of wine Teresa changed places so she could sit next to Amy. 'Helen told me you got pulled over by our sexy sergeant,' she said, bringing her glass up to her lips, her china blue eyes sparkling.

Amy rolled her eyes and reached for her glass of rather dubious red. 'Yes, he did, but fortunately he let me off with a warning.'

'You were lucky. He's not usually so lenient,' Teresa said. 'He's got a real thing about speeding. We've all learned the hard way to keep under the limit. He makes few allowances. Even for friends, not that he gets too close to people. I guess because his plan is to eventually move back to Perth.'

'He doesn't strike me as the friendly type,' Amy commented.

'Angus is certainly a bit reserved,' Teresa said. 'Aloof, if you know what I mean. But, then, some women find that very attractive.'

'Well, I don't.' Amy mentally kicked herself for responding so quickly and emphatically.

Teresa gave her a knowing look that instantly

reminded her of her mother. 'So what made you decide to come all the way out here for three months?' she asked.

Amy shifted her gaze, uncomfortable with concealing the truth about why she had travelled so far. 'I spent the last year in London and felt like I needed to have some breathing space before I decide what to do next. A stint out in the bush seemed like a good idea.'

'This is about as far away as you can get from a big city,' Teresa said. 'I'm used to it now but I hated it at first.'

'So why did you come here?'

'My husband is a fitter and turner on a fishing boat,' she said. 'I suppose you know how rich these shores are in terms of fishing. He's away a lot on the boat, but now the kids are grown up it suits me to work at the clinic to fill in the time.'

'How many kids do you have?'

'Three boys,' Teresa answered with a proud smile. 'They all live in Perth but we see them every couple of months. But what about you? Who have you left pining for you on the other side of the country?'

Amy's mouth twisted. 'No one apart from my

mother,' she said. 'I had a boyfriend a year or so back but he moved on. He's married with a little baby now.'

Teresa winced in empathy. 'That must have hurt.'

'It did but I'm more or less over it now.'

'The change will do you good,' Teresa said wisely. 'You never know, you might like it so much you could end up staying longer. It wouldn't be the first time it's happened.'

Amy looked into the contents of her glass. 'I guess I'll take it one day at a time.'

'Oh, look who's turned up,' Teresa said. 'You must have made an impression after all.'

Amy looked up to lock gazes with Sergeant Angus Ford. She just as quickly looked away again but she could feel the creep of colour seep into her cheeks all the same. She picked up her glass and drained the contents, hoping her head wouldn't punish her for it in the morning.

She watched covertly as Angus approached Bill at the bar, exchanging a few words and accepting what looked like a soda water before he came over to where Teresa made a space for him right next to her.

'What did you do to your eye?' Teresa asked.

'I ran into a drunken door,' he answered dryly.

'How's Carl?' Helen leaned across the table to ask. 'I heard he was on a bit of a bender this afternoon.' Her eyes went to his brow momentarily. 'Looks like he was pretty tanked if you copped that from him.'

'He was, but he's sleeping it off at home now,' he answered. 'I'll go and check on him in the morning.'

'How's your wound feeling?' Amy asked.

His dark brown gaze met hers, a glint of challenge lurking there. 'As you see, I haven't bled to death as yet.'

'You should take care for the next few days,' she said, her mouth pursing slightly. 'The slightest knock can make head wounds bleed a lot.'

'I've got it under control.'

Amy wasn't quite sure how it happened but suddenly it seemed as if everyone else had moved away, leaving her alone with him. She felt the awkward silence nudge her for inspiration but for the life of her couldn't think of a single thing to fill it.

'Would you like another drink?' Angus asked.

Amy was caught off guard. Her eyes flicked to

her empty glass and back to his, but before she could say a word he had got to his feet and spoken to Bill. He came back with a glass of something that looked a whole lot smoother than what she'd been drinking and set it down in front of her.

'I figured since you're staying upstairs you won't drink and drive,' he said.

'Thank you,' she said, and stiffening in affront added, 'But just for the record, I don't drink and drive.'

He ignored her comment to inform her, 'Bill keeps the good stuff out the back. You don't look like the cask type.'

She picked up the glass and sent him a pointed look. 'I thought you had something already planned for this evening.'

He inspected the slice of lemon in his glass before meeting her eyes, his dark gaze all of a sudden very direct and cop-like. 'Why didn't you tell me you were Lindsay Redgrove's cousin?' he asked. 'In fact, why have you not told anyone?'

Amy felt the colour drain from her face. Her fingers holding her glass gave a betraying tremble and her stomach felt as if it had been sucked of all its contents, the sudden hollowness making her feel faint. 'I can't imagine how you came by that information,' she said by way of stalling.

He leaned back in his chair in an indolent manner. 'I'm a cop. I make it my business to know everything about everyone who drifts into town.'

'So you're the control freak I first assumed,' she said. 'I knew it the minute I met you. Exerting public power is important to people like you because you lack it in your personal life.'

He lifted one shoulder in a shrug that indicated it didn't bother him in the least what she thought of him. 'It seems rather a coincidence that you've taken this temporary post,' he said. 'Weren't you satisfied with the coroner's verdict on your cousin's death?'

Amy was wary about revealing her concerns to anyone, and in particular to one of the police officers who had investigated the death of her cousin. She hadn't even gone as far as admitting them to herself. Lindsay had been a suicide threat ever since her first attempt at the age of seventeen, but as the senior officer in town it seemed Angus Ford would be the last person she would be able to confide in. He would have overseen the

CIB and forensics investigation and sent his report to the coroner.

'I hadn't seen Lindsay for three years or so,' she said. 'She wrote to me once or twice and told me she loved it here. I wanted to visit the place where she had found the most happiness and I guess to pay my last respects.'

'You didn't go to her memorial service.'

Amy wasn't sure if he had stated a fact, asked a question or delivered a criticism. 'No,' she said. 'I was unable to get back from London in time.'

He leaned back in his chair, the ice cubes in his glass rattling together slightly. 'It was a nice ceremony,' he said. 'She would have liked it.'

Her eyes flared with surprise. '*You* went to my cousin's funeral?'

He gave a brief nod. 'I had to fly to Sydney on another matter so it was a chance to kill two birds…' His mouth twisted ruefully, 'Sorry— wrong choice of words. It was a chance to pay my respects.'

'How well did you know Lindsay?' she asked.

'As well as anyone else around here did,' he answered. 'She was a loner, didn't seem to need people around her. She was mostly aloof and unreachable unless she wanted to connect with someone, but even then it was always only a temporary thing.'

'Like you?' Amy found herself asking, recalling Helen's words about him, which he had practically used verbatim.

His black-brown unspeaking gaze prolonged the silence, making the tension in the air crackle between them.

'You're rather quick to make character assessments, aren't you, Dr Tanner?' he said with a derisive twist to his mouth. 'You only met me…what is it now…three or four hours ago and you think you've got me all figured out.'

'I know enough about body language to be able to read the "Keep Away" sign you have permanently etched on your face,' she retorted.

The right side of his mouth tipped up even more mockingly. '"Keep Away" sign, huh?'

'Yes.' She straightened her spine and sent him a fixed glare. 'You don't trust people, particularly women.'

'I'm a cop,' he said, running his eyes over her in an assessing manner. 'It's my job to be suspicious.'

'Not everyone is a criminal.'

'Perhaps not. But everyone is a potential one, don't you agree?' he said.

'No, of course I don't agree,' she said. 'I know plenty of people who've never done a single thing wrong.'

He pushed his drink to one side and, leaning his forearms on the table separating them, looked deep into her eyes. 'What about you, Dr Tanner?' he asked in a low velvety tone that sent an unexpected trickling hot river of sensation racing up her spine. 'Are you trying to tell me you've never done a single thing wrong in the whole of your life?'

Amy could feel the brush of his knees against hers beneath the table, the intimate contact sending shooting sparks of heat between her thighs. She looked into that fathoms-deep gaze and felt her stomach give a little quiver of unruly desire. It was unlike anything that had ever happened to her before. She had never felt such a powerful physical attraction for anyone so instantly, and what made it all the more bewildering was he was exactly the type of man she had effectively avoided for most of her life. She didn't even like him and he clearly felt the same towards her if the derisive glint in his eyes was to be taken at face value.

'I'm the first to admit I'm not perfect,' she said. 'But I try to be a good citizen, as indeed I believe the majority of people do.'

'Most people, given the opportunity to stretch the boundaries, do so, particularly if they think there's a chance they're going to get away with it,' he said.

'So what about you, Sergeant Ford?' she asked. 'What laws have *you* been tempted to break recently?'

His smouldering gaze travelled slowly, *very* slowly from her eyes to her mouth, and down to the hint of cleavage her close-fitting white top revealed, before doing the return journey with the same lazy indolence. Amy felt as if she may as well have been sitting there stark naked. Her breasts tightened, their peaks thrusting against the stretch fabric of her top, her skin feathering all over with acute awareness of his undisguised male appraisal.

He leant back in his chair, his eyes tethering hers once more. 'I generally try to stay out of trouble,' he said. 'But very occasionally I'm tempted to step over one of my personal boundaries.'

'What sort of boundaries do you mean?' she

asked. 'Putting your foot down when no one's looking, parking in a loading zone?'

'No, nothing like that,' he answered. 'More intimate ones.'

Amy sent her tongue out to moisten her suddenly parchment-dry lips. 'Like what? Having a one-night stand or something?' she asked.

His eyes glinted with something that made her toes instantly curl. 'Is that a proposition, Dr Tanner?' he asked.

She felt her face flare with scorching heat. 'No, of course not!' she said. 'What sort of person do you think I am? I don't even like you.'

'Liking someone has very little to do with sexual attraction,' he said with another one of his stomach-flipping looks.

Amy couldn't recall a time when she had felt more flustered and out of her depth. 'Just where do you get off, Sergeant?' she asked with caustic bite. 'If you think I'm the least bit interested in becoming involved with an arrogant control freak such as yourself then you really need to have some emergency liposuction done on your overweight ego.'

His sudden laugh nearly made her fall off her

chair. It was so unexpected and so very masculine she felt her heart kick in response to the deep, rich sound of it. His lingering smile—the first one she'd seen on his face—totally transformed his features. His eyes crinkled up at the corners, and his cleanly shaven jaw relaxed, giving him a playful air that was devastatingly attractive.

'It's been quite a while since a woman's been able to make me laugh,' he said, still smiling. 'Congratulations.'

She felt an answering smile tug at her mouth but wouldn't allow it purchase and sent him a reproachful glare instead. 'I feel insulted that you assumed I'd jump into bed with you just because you're relatively good-looking.'

Angus couldn't help grinning at her frowning look. She was certainly a cute little thing with her flashing dark blue eyes and pouting mouth. He felt the tightening in his groin when one of her knees bumped his underneath the table, and smiled to himself when he felt her move away as if he had burnt her.

'Only relatively good-looking, huh?' he asked, stretching his legs beneath the table again.

She rolled her eyes at him and shifted even further backwards in her chair. 'I'm not going to force-feed your ego, I'm sure it gets enough nourishment from all the other women in town.'

He didn't answer but sat watching her as she lifted her glass to her lips. Amy felt self-conscious under his scrutiny, her cheeks still felt hot and her skin suddenly felt too tight for her body. She was shocked at her reaction to him. Her body seemed to have a mind of its own when it was anywhere near his. She could feel the thrum of her pulse beneath her skin, her stomach giving little sharp kicks every time his legs brushed against hers.

Was he doing it deliberately? she wondered. She sneaked a glance at him as she reached for her drink but his face had gone all cop-like again, although there was a hint of a smile lurking about his sensual mouth. She wondered what it would feel like to have that mouth on hers, to feel the probe of his tongue, the rasp of his unshaven jaw on her...

Amy was jerked away from her traitorous thoughts when Bill Huxley came over and removed Angus's empty soda-water glass. 'How about a light beer, Sarge?' he asked. 'Surely you've earned it after this afternoon's drama.'

'No, thanks, Bill,' he said. 'I'm on the light stuff tonight.'

'Are you on call?' Amy asked once Bill had left to gather empty glasses from the other tables.

'No, one of the constables is on tonight. I just have to see to something out at the Cove before I head home.'

'Do you mean Caveside Cove?'

He gave a brief nod.

'Helen was telling me that's where my cousin lived,' she said. 'I had always sent her letters via the post office but I thought I might go out and have a look around some time.'

The unreadable mask settled back down on his features like a curtain coming down on a stage. 'There's nothing out there,' he said. 'It's little more than a lean-to full of spiders and junk. You wouldn't last a minute if this afternoon's arachnophobia routine was any indication.'

'Well, all the same I want to see where Lindsay spent her time,' she said, doing her best to ignore his jibe. 'And her last day…'

'I would advise against it, Dr Tanner. It won't

bring her back, and visiting the scene of where a suicide took place can be very distressing, even for distant relatives.'

Amy frowned at him in indignation. 'I'm not a distant relative! She was my only cousin.'

'Whom you never once visited in the whole time she was here,' he said with more than a hint of reproach.

'I was training to be a doctor, for goodness' sake,' she protested. 'And it's a very long way to come. Besides I couldn't afford the time.'

'You can't have been that close to her,' he said. 'She never once mentioned you.'

Amy's resentment rose inside her, bubbling hot. 'She was a very private person, that's why,' she said. 'You said it yourself.'

'Even very private people occasionally mention the most important people in their life.'

'Oh, really?' She arched one brow at him. 'Let's test that little theory of yours, shall we? How about you, Sergeant Ford? You're a private and aloof person—who are the most important people in your life?'

He held her challenging look for several

pulsing seconds, making Amy wonder if he was even going to bother to answer.

'My parents, who live in Perth, are important to me,' he finally said.

'Any brothers or sisters?' she asked.

'No, I'm an only child.'

'Is there a woman in your life?' she asked.

There was a tiny, almost undetectable pause.

'Not at present.'

'So that's it?' She frowned at him. 'Your parents and no one else?'

'I have a dog.'

She let out a cynical laugh. 'Yeah, well, I guess that makes sense.'

'What do you mean by that?' he asked, his eyes narrowing slightly.

Amy felt her skin prickle at his tone. 'What sort of dog have you got?' she asked. 'I bet it's not a teacup Chihuahua. '

His top lip lifted slightly. 'He's a German shepherd.'

'That figures as well,' she said. 'You can always tell a person by their dog.'

'What kind of comment is that, Dr Tanner?' He

laughed mockingly. 'Perhaps you have something against dogs?'

'I have no problem with dogs,' she returned. 'It's the owners I take issue with. I've seen too many dog attacks on small children to be under any illusions about controlling a large dog. They're instinctive animals and should never be trusted.'

'Are you talking about men or dogs?' Angus countered, stretching his legs again.

Her chair squeaked along the floor as she inched back a fraction. 'You think I have some sort of hang-up about men, don't you?' she said with a withering look.

He laid one arm along the back of the neighbouring chair, the action making his biceps bulge as he met her flashing eyes. 'You have all the signs of a woman recently spurned,' he said.

Amy felt her face glow with betraying colour. 'That's not true,' she spluttered. *Well, it was sort of true,* she had to admit, although not to him. Eighteen months was fairly recent, wasn't it?

His expression indicated he didn't believe her for a second.

She threw him an accusing glare. 'I suppose

you've had me investigated or something, have you? Interviewed a few past boyfriends, got an update on my social life? Is that how you found out I was Lindsay's cousin? Did you run a background check on me?'

'No,' he said. 'I remember your aunt mentioning your name. She also showed me a photo—one that put your licence photo to shame.'

'Oh…' Amy felt herself backing down. She toyed with her drink, wondering if she should just finish it and move on, but something about his summation of her so far intrigued her. How on earth had he guessed about Simon if he hadn't done some sort of check? Was she really giving off such easy-to-read signals? she wondered. Her mother had told her repeatedly to put Simon's betrayal behind her but she had been too busy to even think about dating again.

In fact, up until now she hadn't even been the slightest bit tempted…

'I suppose you know I'm sailing a bit close to the wind on my licence,' she inserted into the silence.

'I did happen to notice that,' he said. 'But don't expect any favours from me out here, Dr Tanner.

You might need to drive for your job, but one strike and you're out.'

She tightened her mouth. 'You'd do it, wouldn't you?'

'I'm here to uphold the law and if you're breaking it then naturally we're going to clash.'

Her lip curled contemptuously. 'You remind me of someone I once knew,' she said. 'He never missed a chance to point out a misdemeanour, real or imagined.'

'I take it that would be your father?' he asked.

She stared at him in shock. Had he a sixth sense or what? 'Don't tell me,' she said when she had regained her composure. 'I show the classic signs of a daughter with father issues, right?'

'It seems to me you have issues with men— period.'

Amy decided to swing the conversation back to safer ground. 'You said you were only close to your parents and your dog, but what about your work colleagues?' she asked. 'I would have thought you'd get rather close to them working side by side each day, at times under very trying circumstances.'

'That's to some degree true but it's not always

wise to get too attached. It can interfere with how you view their work if you have too close an attachment to them.'

She screwed up her mouth at him. 'You really have cynicism down to an art, don't you?'

'I'm a realist, Dr Tanner,' he said. 'I've seen too much to be under any illusions about human nature.'

'What do your parents do for a living?' she asked, suddenly keen to find out more about what had contributed to his skewed world view.

'My father was a cop like me but is now retired, and my mother manages a child-care centre. She says it's her way of compensating for the lack of grandchildren.'

'You don't want kids at some point?'

'At some point, yes, but first I have to find a woman who can cope with the long hours I work without nagging me all the time to consider a career change.' He sent her a small rueful smile. 'Not an easy task, I can assure you.'

Amy sensed there was a world of information in his comment about his previous relationships with women. In spite of her negative experiences with her father, she knew being a cop was a tough call and contributed to a lot of stress and relationship breakdowns.

'My father was a cop, too,' she said. 'But, then, I suppose you've already guessed that.'

'I had noticed you don't seem to like cops all that much.'

'Yeah, well, I don't like my father all that much so that more or less explains it, I guess,' she said.

'What about your mother?'

'She's great,' Amy said with a glimmer of a smile. 'A bit overprotective and full-on at times, but we're really close. She's a vet. I used to help her in the practice when I was a kid.'

'So how come you chose medicine instead?'

She sent him a quick there-one-second-gone-the-next smile. 'Dealing with animals was too frustrating for me. They can't tell you their symptoms so you're always left guessing. I much prefer to deal with humans who can at least tell me what they're feeling.'

'Dogs can do that, too,' he said. 'I know every one of Fergus's moods.'

'So that's his name,' she said. 'It's not very Germanic, is it?'

'No, but it's the name of a loyal friend I once had,' he said. 'I thought it was appropriate.'

She looked at him with a questioning glance. *'Had?'*

He rose from his chair in a single movement, his tall shadow falling over her like a warning. 'I'd better get going,' he said. 'I have some things to see to. No doubt I'll see you around.'

Amy's brow furrowed as he strode out of the pub, his long purposeful strides taking him and his closely guarded secrets out of her reach.

CHAPTER FOUR

AMY'S first morning at the clinic started with meeting the other GP in the practice, Allan Peddington, a man in his late sixties who looked like he had done too many nights on call.

'I'm sorry I wasn't here to meet you yesterday,' he said, briefly shaking her hand. 'I had a family emergency down in Geraldton.'

'That's fine,' she said, smiling at him reassuringly. 'I hope everything's OK with your family now.'

Allan's tired eyes spoke volumes. 'Yes, more or less, I think,' he said. 'But you never know with kids, they seem right one minute and the next they're running off the rails. My daughter Claire is not coping too well after a break-up with her live-in partner. They were supposed to be getting married in a few months. It's such a disappointment for her.'

'I'm so sorry,' she said. 'It must be very hard for you, and your wife as well.'

'My wife died a few years ago,' he said in a flat emotionless tone that didn't fool Amy for a second. 'There's just Claire and me now.'

'I'm sorry,' she said. 'I didn't realise.'

He gave her a forced smile. 'Well, we'd better get on with the day. Helen told me she showed you around yesterday. It's a one in two on call but if you have anything special planned any time, just let me know and I'll fill in for you.'

'And likewise,' Amy offered, although for the life of her couldn't imagine what would crop up for her to do in the evenings in a place as small as this.

Her first patient was a young man in his early twenties who had been welding the day before, and presented with a foreign object in his right eye.

'It hurts like hell, my eye's watering and it feels like there's sand under my eyelid,' Josh Taylor complained as he got up on the table and lay back as Amy had directed. 'I should have done something about it yesterday but I had to get the job done for the boss.'

She inspected the eye under a bright light. 'It

looks like you've got a metal fragment lodged on the surface of your cornea,' she said. 'I'll put some anaesthetic drops in your eye and remove it for you, but next time you really shouldn't wait when something like this happens. You could have developed an ulcer, which is much harder to treat.'

'I know, but I've only been working in this job a short time and I didn't want the boss to think I was slacking off,' he said.

After Amy reassured herself that Josh was not using powerful enough equipment to have caused an intraocular foreign body, which would have required a trip to Geraldton and an ocular X-ray, she put three drops of proxymetacaine into his eye and waited for a couple of minutes, chatting to him about his work. She found out he worked for one of the fishermen in town as a general deckhand and that he had family further north in Broome.

'OK, now keep very still,' she said. 'I know it can seem a bit weird looking at a needle coming towards your eye but you won't feel a thing.'

She took a 22-gauge needle and, donning a pair of magnifying glasses and steadying her arm on a rest, she approached the cornea from the side. She could see the irritating metal fragment and with great care pried off the object with the tip of the needle. Then she applied some chloromycetin ointment and a double pad to the eye.

'You'll need to leave the pad in place for the rest of the day and night to protect your eye. Once the anaesthetic drops wear off you'll probably feel as if something is still in there, but that's because you've scratched the surface of the cornea. It will feel better in a day or so. I'd like to see you tomorrow to make sure it's healing well.'

'Thanks, Dr Tanner,' he said with a grateful smile. 'Hey, you know something? You look too young to be a doctor.'

She gave him an exaggerated smile and opened the door. 'You're seeing me with one eye, Josh,' she said. 'I might look old enough to be your mother when you come back tomorrow.'

There was a five-minute break in the appointment book so Amy dashed out to the general store to buy a snack for morning tea. She had forgone breakfast at the hotel, deciding that the bacon and eggs and sausages on the menu weren't going to do her thighs any favours.

She came out of the store, her head down against the glare of the hot bright sunshine, and cannoned straight into a blue-uniformed, rock-hard chest.

'Oops…' she said as strong male arms steadied her. 'Sorry, I wasn't watching where I was going.'

'In a hurry again, Dr Tanner?' Angus asked with a tilt of his mouth.

Amy rolled her lips together in disapproval at his little jibe. 'I missed breakfast,' she said. 'I've only got five minutes between patients.'

His hands fell away from her upper arms, but Amy could still feel her flesh tingling. Her stomach did a funny little somersault as his gaze went to her mouth before returning to her eyes.

'How's your first day on the job?' he asked.

'Fine,' she said with a little toss of her head. 'Nothing I can't handle.'

'So far,' he drawled.

Amy gave him a brittle look and made to brush past him, but he counteracted it with a hand on her arm. She looked down at his strong tanned fingers against the lighter tone of her slim wrist, a feathery sensation running up her spine as she brought her gaze upwards to meet his. 'Am I under arrest, Sergeant Ford?' she asked in a pert tone.

'Is there any reason why you should be under arrest, Dr Tanner?' he asked as he released her.

'I haven't done anything wrong,' she said with a hitch of her chin.

He rocked back on his heels as he looked down at her. 'So far.'

She gave him one last blistering look and stomped across the road back to the clinic, clutching her apple and tub of low-fat yogurt.

Angus squinted against the bright sunlight as he watched her, a slow smile spreading across his face.

'Is that the new doctor?' Jonathon Upton asked as he got out of his dusty utility in front of the store.

'G'day, Jonno,' Angus said, flicking a quick glance his way before returning to the little figure who'd had to wait in the middle of the street for a car to pass. 'Yep, that's her all right.'

Jonno whistled through his teeth as he followed the line of Angus's dark brown gaze. 'Damn nice figure,' he said. 'What's she like as a person?'

Angus wrenched his gaze away from the other

side of the street. He put his sunglasses on and
gave the farmer a tight-lipped, on-off smile. 'She
drives too fast,' he said, and walked back to the
police station.

'So how was your first morning?' Helen asked
as Amy came out after seeing another patient.

'Not bad,' she said handing her a pile of files.
'It's a bit of change from working in a city
hospital, of course, but to tell you the truth, it's
a bit of a relief to be away from all that pressure.'

'Oh, it can get pretty pressured out here at
times,' Helen said, pulling out the filing cabinet
drawer. 'You just wait until there's a major
accident on the highway or something. You can
get called out at any time of the night to attend.
And Friday and Saturday nights can get a bit
lively. The young ones are bored and drink too
much and get into all sorts of trouble.'

'I suppose kids will kick up their heels
wherever they live,' Amy said thinking of her
own teenage years.

'It's hard, though, in isolated areas,' Helen said.
'I've heard stories of kids petrol-sniffing in some
communities further north, which just adds to the

on-going problem of alcohol abuse. We haven't had anything like that out here yet, but I have a friend who lives in Perth whose daughter nearly died after taking ecstasy. The party drug scene in some places is really scary. I certainly hope it doesn't get like that out here. We don't have the infrastructure in these country areas to deal with drug abuse. It'll be left to the families to deal with, there's no drug counselling or rehab facilities out here.'

'What about educational programmes at the local schools?' Amy suggested. 'That might prevent the problem from starting in the first place.'

'We don't have a senior high school here, only kindergarten to year ten. Sergeant Ford's done a couple of lectures but you know what kids are like—particularly boys—with people in positions of authority, especially those in uniform. He decided to try another tactic instead. He coaches a soccer team on Tuesday afternoons. One or two of the tough kids have started coming along. Mixing with the others seems to be helping. There's been a lot less petty crime since.'

'That does sound like a good tactic,' Amy said,

privately impressed with Angus's initiative in spite of her annoyance towards him.

'You should go down after your clinic finishes this afternoon and watch them,' Helen suggested. 'They play on the oval a few blocks down from the pub. It will be a way to get to know some of the lads, most of whom will no doubt turn out to be your patients at one time or the other.'

'I might just do that,' Amy said. 'Soccer's one of my favourite games.'

'You never know, Sergeant Ford might even let you have a kick or two,' Helen said with a twinkling smile. 'I saw the two of you chatting like old friends last night. Could there be a hint of romance in the air?'

'You must be joking,' Amy said, perhaps a little too quickly to be convincing. 'He's *so* not my type, for one thing…'

'And the other thing?' Helen prompted.

'I'm only here for three months,' she said, more to remind herself than the receptionist. 'I'm not interested in temporary relationships. I'm not that sort of woman.'

'All the same, it wouldn't hurt to have a little fun while you're out here,' Helen advised. 'It can be a lonely place without some company in the evenings.'

'I have plenty of company at the hotel,' Amy said, recalling how she'd spent most of the night twitching with fear in case her hairy roommate returned, not to mention the noise from the pub downstairs before it finally closed for the night.

Helen gave a little snort as she reached for the next patient's file just as the front door of the clinic opened. 'You might not be so positive come Friday or Saturday night. That place can really jump and let me tell you—it ain't pretty.'

Amy didn't answer but turned to greet the next patient. 'Mrs Horsham?'

Gillian Horsham followed her and took the chair Amy offered her in her consulting room, her eyes slightly downcast as she twisted her thin hands together in her lap.

'What can I do for you, Mrs Horsham?' Amy asked.

'I keep getting headaches,' Gillian said.

Amy felt like rolling her eyes in frustration. How many middle-aged women were there in the world with headaches? she wondered. It was every GP's nightmare. She glanced down at the thick file of notes, her eyes widening at how many tests had already been carried out with no specific diagnosis. It had quite clearly been both Allan Peddington's and Jacqui Ridley's nightmare as well.

'Describe to me what your headache feels like,' Amy said. 'Is it a slow build-up, or a rapid onset, do you get blurred vision or nausea?'

'No…just a headache…'

'Is it centred over one or both of your eyes or somewhere else?' Amy asked.

'I don't know…it's just there…' She pointed vaguely to her head.

Amy reached for the blood-pressure machine. 'I'll start with your blood pressure first as that can sometimes cause headaches,' she said. 'Are you currently on any medication?'

'No,' Gillian said, wincing slightly as Amy pumped up the cuff over the thin cotton of the sleeve of her blouse on her upper arm.

'Is that hurting?' she asked.

'No, I guess I did too much in the garden yesterday.'

Amy frowned as she measured the woman's blood pressure: 120 over 70, as expected—

normal. After a thorough physical examination, which excluded papilloedema, cranial nerve deficits or other neurological signs, Amy was left without a physical diagnosis.

'I can't find any signs of disease on examination. You've had some basic bloods done in the past, but I'll run a couple of more specific blood tests on you to check thyroid and parathyroid function,' she said, and reached for the blood-collection trolley. She searched for a vein in Gillian's arm and, finding one, drew up sufficient blood before placing a circular sticking plaster on the puncture site. 'Don't lift anything heavy with that arm for an hour or so,' Amy instructed her. 'The results should be back in a few days so make another appointment on your way out.'

'Thank you, Doctor,' Gillian said, and got to her feet. 'I know the other doctors think it's all in my mind but I do feel unwell a lot of the time. I have for years.'

'I'll do my best to find out what's causing your headaches,' Amy promised as she walked with her back out to Reception.

Helen waited until the woman had left before turning to Amy. 'She's a weird one, that,' she said. 'I suppose she came in with a headache or something equally vague?'

Amy frowned. 'Yes, she did, actually. Why, is that commonplace with her?'

'It drove Jacqui crazy,' Helen said. 'She ran every test known to medical science on that woman and came up with nothing. Allan did, too. Gillian Horsham is basically a bored housewife. She sits in front of her computer all day searching the internet for new symptoms. She knows more about rare diseases than a university professor. She's lonely. Her only daughter lives in America. She comes in for attention, regular as clockwork, at least once a month, sometimes more.'

Amy handed Helen the blood specimen for pathology with a slightly embarrassed look. 'I guess I have a lot to learn about the locals,' she said.

Helen patted her hand. 'You'll soon get the hang of it.'

CHAPTER FIVE

AMY hadn't really intended going down to the oval, but the hotel bar was crowded and the noise deafening when she went up to her room, so she put on her trainers, shorts and a T-shirt and told herself she was going for a walk to blow away the cobwebs. She gave a little shiver and amended quickly—the *dust* of the day.

The heat was as intense as ever, the sun burning through the light cotton of her top as she walked past the police station towards the oval.

She could hear the sound of young male voices calling out to each other and the deeper voice of Angus Ford as he issued instructions. She stood in the shade of the dilapidated grandstand and watched as the boys went through some kicking drills. She couldn't help noticing how athletic Angus looked in his shorts and lightweight muscle top. His upper body was obviously used to some sort of regular and strenuous workout if his well-formed muscles were any indication, and his legs too looked as if they were well used to being pushed to the limits of endurance.

He looked magnificent.

A loud wolf-whistle suddenly cut through the air. 'Hey, Jake, Matt, have a look at that!' one young boy called out.

Angus turned his head and that same slight hint of annoyance she'd seen the night before showed briefly in his dark eyes as they met hers. He turned away again and addressed the young men under his tutelage. 'Just keep on with that training drill for a couple of minutes. I won't be long.'

'Is she your new girlfriend, Sarge?' the boy who had delivered the wolf-whistle asked with a cheeky grin.

'You've *got* to be joking,' Angus said, and came over to where Amy was now silently seething.

She gave him an arch look. *'You've got to be joking?'* She mimicked his deep, scathing tone.

'I thought that might get a rise out of you,' he said. 'What can I do for you, Dr Tanner?'

'I didn't come here to see *you,*' she said with

a little toss of her head. 'I came to see the boys playing.'

'They can probably do without the distraction,' he said as his eyes dipped to where her breasts pushed against her top.

She folded her arms across her chest but all it did was give him an even better view of her cleavage. 'If I'm not welcome, I'll leave,' she bit out.

'I didn't mean to imply that.'

'Oh, yes, you did,' she said. 'But while I'm here, there is something I want to ask you.'

'My head wound, as you see, is fine.'

'It's not about your wound,' she said. 'I have something else I wish to discuss with you.'

He stood with his arms folded, rocking back on his heels slightly as he looked down at her. 'Let me guess, you've been speeding and want to confess.'

She sent him a frosty look. 'Must you be so…so annoying?'

'Just doing my job, Dr Tanner.'

She drew in a tight breath and asked, 'Have you told anyone else in town that I am Lindsay's cousin?'

'No.'

She frowned. 'Why not?'

'I kind of figured you didn't want anyone to know,' he said. 'If you had, you would have mentioned it from the first.'

Amy compressed her lips for a moment. 'You're right,' she said, blowing out a little breath. 'I don't really want people to know.'

'Your reasons being?'

'I wasn't sure how well liked she was,' she answered, thinking on her feet as she continued, 'Mental illness is still not properly understood in the community and probably less so in one as isolated as this one. I didn't want to have to deal with any prejudice.'

'So you don't want to be associated with her, is that right?' There was an element of censure in his tone. 'Too embarrassing for you to have a not-quite-normal relative, eh, *Dr* Tanner?'

Amy ground her teeth and held her hands stiffly by her sides. 'That's not what I said.'

'Isn't it?' His dark brown eyes challenged hers.

'No.'

'So what *are* you saying, Dr Tanner?'

'I told you last night. I wanted to visit Lindsay's home and community,' she said.

'But you don't want anyone to know who you are.'

'I don't think it's relevant,' she said. 'Besides, grief is a very private and personal thing.'

'Undoubtedly, but you don't strike me as particularly grief-stricken,' he said.

'And I suppose you're an expert on analysing the depth of grief people show, are you, Sergeant?' she said with increasing temper. 'Running it through your own little grief meter to see if it's genuine or not? Well, let me tell you that there are different ways of showing grief. Not everybody does it with copious amounts of tears at the mere mention of the loved one's name.'

'That's certainly true, but I can't help thinking you're not telling me the whole story behind your pilgrimage to Marraburra,' he said.

'I don't have to explain myself to you,' she flashed back.

Angus opened his mouth to respond but there was a sound of a hard thud and a rough swear word, closely followed by a groan of agony on the oval behind him. He turned to see Matt Healey stumbling, as white as a sheet, clutching his left shoulder.

'Matt? What happened?' he asked, rushing over.

'It's my shoulder,' Matt groaned. 'I ran into Jake and something went crack.'

Amy was close behind Angus and offered to help. 'Matt, let me have a look,' she said. 'Where does it hurt?'

'It hurts like hell…' Matt said, biting his lip in an effort to keep control in front of his mates.

Amy gently examined the shoulder, seeing through the singlet top the typical flattening of the front contour of the joint due to dislocation. Feeling the area confirmed her diagnosis. Fortunately his sensation over the shoulder was normal, indicating he hadn't damaged any sensory nerves.

'Matt I'm afraid you've dislocated your shoulder,' she said. 'We'll have to get it back in place but it's going to be too painful to do it here. It'll be much better if we can get you back to the medical clinic and give you some sedation. But we'll need to contact your parents first.'

Matt exchanged a quick glance with Angus before looking at Amy again. 'I live with my dad but he's out on a boat. I'm not sure if his mobile will be on.'

'What about your mother? Can she be contacted?' Amy asked.

'I'll contact Matt's mother,' Angus said. Turning to the rest of the team, he went on, 'Sorry guys, we'll have to finish there for today. I'll try and make some time later in the week, perhaps Thursday. I'll let Jake know.'

'Good luck, Matt,' the boys chorused.

A tall dark-haired, dark-skinned boy came over to Matt, his expression sheepish. 'Sorry, Matt,' he mumbled. 'I didn't mean to hurt you, mate.'

Matt's smile was more of a grimace. 'It's all right, Jake. You did me a favour. I won't have to do the English test tomorrow.'

Amy turned to Angus. 'Have you got your car nearby? I know it's not far to the clinic but that shoulder will be killing him and the sooner it's put back in the better.'

'I'll jog over and get it—won't be a minute,' Angus said, and rushed off.

'Come over here into the shade,' Amy said, leading the boy towards the shadow of the grandstand.

'Sorry, Doc,' Matt said with another twisted grimace. 'You'd probably finished for the day.'

'It's no problem, Matt,' she said with a smile. 'It's just a shame you had such a freak accident. It can take a while for a dislocated shoulder to heal. You'll have to take things easy for a while.'

'You mean I won't be able to train?'

She shook her head. 'Not for a couple of weeks. Maybe you can run, but just not use the shoulder. The good news is in most cases the shoulder returns to normal.'

Amy looked up to see Angus pull into the kerb closest to the grandstand and she led Matt towards the car.

'Better sit in the front, Matt,' Angus said, holding the door open. 'I've phoned your mother and she's on her way down now.'

'Thanks, Sarge. I hope she wasn't too upset,' Matt said.

Angus gave him a man-to man smile. 'You know what mothers are like—it's their job to be upset.'

It was a short journey to the clinic and Amy led them inside to the main treatment room, where Teresa was the nurse on duty.

'So what have you been doing to yourself, Mattie?' she asked.

'Popped my shoulder,' he said with a rueful look. 'The doctor's going to put it back in.'

'Has Matt's mother arrived yet?' Amy asked.

'*Matthew!*' A distraught female voice suddenly echoed through the building and Matt rolled his eyes.

'Looks like it,' Teresa said with a knowing wink towards the blushing boy. 'I'll bring her in.'

Rowena Healey was crying as she came in and would have crushed her son in a hug except for Amy anticipating it and blocking her. 'It's all right, Mrs Healey,' she said reassuringly. 'Matt's got a dislocated shoulder and I need your permission to administer an IV sedative to relax him while I reposition it. Could you sign the consent form Teresa has? Then we'll get it done.'

'Oh, my poor baby…' Rowena sobbed as she signed the form with a trembling hand.

'*Mu-um,*' Matt groaned in embarrassment.

Amy looked at Angus. 'Could you help Matt onto the bed, please?'

'Sure.'

Once Matt was lying on the bed Amy prepared his hand for an IV canula, with Teresa standing nearby in case of any problems with airway. She injected some midazolam, which almost immediately took effect and relaxed the teenager.

'Sergeant Ford, could you put your arms under Matt's shoulders like this to stop him from sliding from the bed?' she asked, demonstrating the position.

'Like this?' Angus asked.

'Exactly like that,' Amy said, and for the benefit of the witnesses added pleasantly, 'You must have done this before.'

'Yeah,' he answered, holding her gaze for a fraction longer than was needed.

Amy bent Matt's elbow to ninety degrees and, pulling downwards on the arm, rotated the shoulder joint to the front. With a clunk the joint popped back into place.

'I'll put his shoulder into a collar and cuff,' Amy said to Matt's mother, who was hovering anxiously. 'And if you could make sure he has some paracetomol four-hourly for pain, and keep him resting, I'll see him tomorrow in the clinic.'

'Can I take him home now?' Rowena asked.

'Wait here half an hour till the sedation wears off a bit,' Amy said. 'He's still groggy but that will be a good thing for a few minutes. Let's sit him up in one of the armchairs in the waiting area.'

'I'll help you out with him,' Angus said to the boy's mother.

Amy stood back as Angus escorted the boy out with his mother, supporting him gently but firmly to get him settled into a comfortable chair.

Teresa tidied up the treatment bay, commenting over her shoulder, 'He's done a wonder with that kid, you know.'

Amy pretended an interest in the suture and bandage trolley, her tone offhand as she answered, 'Oh?'

'Yeah,' the nurse said. 'Matt was up on three shoplifting charges all before the age of thirteen, not to mention under-age drinking when he was fourteen and driving an unlicensed vehicle without a licence at fifteen. But look at him now. He's not long turned sixteen and he's one of the nicest kids around here.'

Amy turned to look at the nurse. 'So how do you attribute that to Sergeant Ford's influence?' she asked.

'Angus spends time with the lads around here,' Teresa said. 'In fact, he spends more time with some of those boys than their own fathers—or at least the few that are still around, that is.' She straightened the bed and added, 'Angus is a good role model for them. He's the best thing that ever happened to this place, I can tell you. The other cops are good enough, don't get me wrong, but Angus has a real heart for youth in isolated areas.'

'He sounds like an angel in cop's clothing,' Amy said with a cynical tilt to her mouth. 'I wonder where he hides his halo.'

'You're very welcome to search me and find out,' Angus said from just behind her.

Amy flushed to the roots of her hair as she swung around, her eyes meeting the sardonic gleam of his. 'I didn't hear you come back in…' she said.

'Obviously.'

'Er…' Teresa cleared her throat. 'I'm about to close up shop now. Allan's on call tonight and so am I if there's any trouble. I'll head off as soon as Matt and his mum are ready to go.'

Amy turned to face the nurse. 'Thanks, Teresa, for helping out. I'll see you tomorrow.'

'Have a good night, both of you,' Teresa said with a twinkle in her eye.

Amy walked out, her face still feeling unbearably hot. She heard Angus following a few paces behind her.

'Do you want a lift back to the hotel?' he asked as they came out from the air-conditioned interior of the clinic.

'I think I can manage to survive the hundred-and-fifty-metre journey without collapsing from dehydration or heatstroke,' she said with a defiant little toss of her head.

A small smile began to play at the edges of his mouth. 'You look like you're overheating right now,' he observed.

She gave him a withering look and made to stalk past but he caught her wrist to stall her. She felt that same quick snap of electricity shoot through her flesh as his long fingers curled around the slender bones of her wrist like a steel handcuff. Her eyes went to his, hers flashing with anger.

'What is it this time, Sergeant? Am I walking too fast for your liking?'

His hand released hers but she could still feel his touch as if he had branded her. Her stomach gave a tiny shuffling movement as his eyes flicked to her mouth before coming back to tether her gaze.

'I was going to suggest you come out to Caveside Cove with me to look at your cousin's shack,' he said. 'That's if you've got nothing better to do right now.'

Amy looked up at him, a hint of suspicion in her expression. 'I thought you said there was nothing out there. "Spiders and junk" were your exact words, if I remember correctly.'

'That's right, but I thought you might like some company, particularly if any spiders get too close and personal,' he said. 'It's not an easy place to find, it's isolated out there, and, besides, I happen to have the only key.'

'I don't need a bodyguard,' she said, still bristling with pride. 'And I'm perfectly able to read a road map.'

'But you don't have a four-wheel-drive vehicle,' he said. 'It's a rough road and if you get into trouble it's a long walk back to town.'

'Oh…' She chewed at her lip for a moment, a small frown forming. 'But…but how did my cousin manage? I didn't think she had a car of any sort—as far as I know, she never learned to drive.'

'She didn't,' he answered. 'She rode her bike to the main road and if anyone she knew was going past she'd leave the bike in the bushes and get a lift the rest of the way, and do the same on the way back.'

Amy was tempted to take him up on his offer but couldn't help wondering why he was offering it the first place. But then the thought of getting her brand new car bogged down in sand or the suspension damaged by deep potholes was enough incentive to push her pride to one side and accept.

'All right,' she said. 'I would like to go and see where she lived if it's not too much trouble for you.'

'No trouble at all,' he said, and led the way to his four-wheel-drive police vehicle. 'Besides, the pub's a pig of a place to be at this time of day.'

'Tell me about it,' she said scathingly as he opened the car door for her.

His eyes met hers. 'If you want to move out I still have that room I was telling you about.'

'Thanks, but so far I'm managing,' she said as she got into the car.

He got behind the wheel and reached the outskirts of town before he spoke again. 'That was a good job you did on Matt Healey.'

'Thank you.'

'He's had a rough time,' he said. 'His mother, as you probably guessed, is the nervous type and his father is away a lot.'

'He's a fisherman, right?'

He nodded. 'Yeah. Off the coast is the continental shelf so there's an abundance of fish. The big boats go out for a couple of weeks at a time so it can be a lonely existence for the women and children left at home, given that there's not much to do in terms of entertainment.'

'How long have you been coaching the boys?' she asked.

'For about a year and a bit now.'

'How long have you been here at Marraburra?'

'Two and a half years,' he said.

She turned to look at him. 'So what brought you way up here?'

He kept his eyes on the road but Amy noticed his hands on the steering-wheel had tightened just enough for the knuckles to go pale beneath his tan.

'I decided it was time for a change,' he said evenly. 'I'd been working on a big case in Perth and after several months it began to take its toll. I was living and breathing work, forgetting to have a life. I'm sure you're familiar with the syndrome.'

'Yes, I am,' she agreed wholeheartedly. 'All work and no play makes for a very burnt-out person. I have to constantly be on guard against it. I guess it's that type-A personality most driven, professional people are lumbered with.'

'So you would describe yourself as driven?' he asked.

'Well…' Amy thought about her reasons for coming all this way. 'Yes, I guess you could say that. I like to see things through to the end. I hate quitting halfway through something.'

'Yeah, well, I guess I'm a bit like that, too.'

'Someone, I think it was one of the nurses, said you weren't planning on staying here in-definitely,' she said. 'What will you do, go back to Perth?'

'Probably,' he said. 'But at the moment I'm taking it one day at a time. When it feels like the right time to go back I will.'

Amy wondered what was keeping him here in Marraburra. The town hardly seemed big enough to warrant four police officers, and even though he had said he had wanted a break from his work in Perth, surely he would have put some sort of time frame on it?

'Do you mind if I make a quick detour to pick up someone?' he asked after a tiny pause.

'No, no, of course not,' Amy answered, not quite understanding why she should be feeling disappointed. It wasn't that she wanted to be alone with him. She didn't even like him. If he wanted to dilute her company then that was perfectly fine with her.

She told herself it was because she wanted to visit Lindsay's shack in solitude.

Yes, that was it.

It couldn't possibly be anything else.

CHAPTER SIX

ANGUS turned into a road marked Marraburra Point and drove up a steep hill to where a large open-plan house overlooked the sparkling blue ocean. The height of the cliffs was breathtaking, and the salty tang of the air rising up from the crawling sea below made Amy long for a swim after the blistering heat of the day.

'Wow!' she said. 'This is a fabulous place your friend has here.'

'Yes, it is,' he said, as he brought the car to a halt in front of the glass and stone residence. 'I'm house-sitting it for the owner, who's living overseas at the moment.'

She swivelled to look at him. 'So who are we picking up?' she asked.

He got out and, putting two fingers into his mouth, whistled once, the sound piercing in spite of the pounding of the surf down below.

Amy watched as a glossy-coated German shepherd appeared as if from nowhere to come to his master, his snout nuzzling against Angus's hand affectionately, the dog's tail wagging in greeting.

'Hi, there, boy,' Angus said ruffling the dog's ears. 'Want to come down to the beach?'

Fergus barked as if he had understood every word and Angus smiled and gave him another quick pat. 'Fergus, this is Dr Tanner. Friend, Fergus, friend.'

Amy stood very still as the dog came over and gave her hand a sniff. 'Hi, there, Fergus…'

'Don't be nervous,' Angus said. 'If he didn't like you he would have shown it by now.'

Unlike his owner, Amy couldn't help thinking as she gave the dog a scratch under the chin. 'Pleased to meet you, Fergus,' she said.

Angus opened the lock-up compartment at the back of the vehicle and with a quick non-verbal command Fergus jumped in and sat down as if he had done it many times.

Amy swung an ironic glance Angus's way as they resumed their seats. 'So how come Fergus has to travel like a criminal in the back?' she asked.

He answered as he turned the car back towards

the exit. 'Unrestrained dogs in vehicles are like missiles if you have to brake suddenly, especially a large dog. It's safer for him and for us if he stays back there.'

Amy couldn't help feeling her mother would approve of Angus's attitude. How many times had Grace Tanner said the very same thing?

'He's a beautiful dog,' she inserted into the silence. 'And obviously adores you.'

His eyes met hers briefly. 'Thanks.'

Amy looked around with interest as Angus turned into a road further along the coast marked Caveside Cove. Banksia, grevillea and melaleuca lined each side of the road and in the distance she could hear the roar of the surf.

The road was as he'd said: rough. She jerked from side to side in her seat in spite of the police vehicle's sophisticated suspension and she inwardly sighed with relief when he finally drew the car to a halt.

'It's a bit of a walk,' he said as she joined him on the track leading to the beach. 'Your cousin's shack is tucked in behind the dunes.'

'It's certainly very private,' Amy said as she fell into step beside him. 'Helen Scott was telling me it's not very popular with the locals. She told me there was a tragic rockfall in the caves some years ago.'

'Yes,' he said, stopping briefly to pick up a piece of driftwood and throwing it for Fergus to fetch. 'The caves have been blocked off ever since. But even without that there's usually a strong undertow here and submerged rocks. If you want a swim it's best to go to Marraburra Bay, closer to town.'

'What about the beach below your place, Marraburra Point?'

His eyes met hers in a quick sideways glance, his expression hard to read. 'It's not for the inexperienced either,' he said.

They continued walking until they came to a rustic-looking one-room shack.

'I'll unlock it for you but do you want me to check for spiders first?' he asked.

Amy searched his face for a moment. She suspected he was still amused by her revulsion for spiders but his tone this time held no trace of mockery. She captured her bottom lip for a fraction of a second before answering softly, 'That would be great.'

She waited for him outside, lifting her face to the fresh air and breathing deeply, relishing in the total peace of the place. No wonder her cousin had loved it so much. The red ochre of the cliffs in the distance and the icing-sugar softness of the sand and the wild untamed sound of the sea all added to the sense of isolation and privacy.

The sound of Angus's footsteps brought her head around and she unconsciously rubbed at her arms. 'Did you find any?'

'I've removed a few tenants but as long as you can cope with cobwebs, it should be all clear for half an hour or so,' he said.

She gave a little shiver as she approached the door. 'Cobwebs are OK as long as they stay out of my hair.'

His eyes met hers as he held the door open for her. 'You really are scared, aren't you?'

'I've had some treatment for it,' she confessed. 'But, as you can see, it wasn't entirely successful. My Harley Street psychologist would be terribly disappointed in me.'

His gaze shifted away from hers. 'Yeah, well, they don't always have all the answers so I wouldn't let it worry you.'

There was something in his comment that alerted her to the possibility that he had spent time with a counsellor himself, but she didn't feel comfortable asking him for details. He had his 'keep out' sign on his face again, but when she met his eyes once more she couldn't help thinking they looked too old for his face, as if they'd seen things they hadn't wanted to see and now couldn't erase.

She stepped into the room and tried to keep her eyes from darting nervously about, but it was almost impossible not to be on edge in the badly lit, dusty room. In spite of the heat burning its way into the shack she felt a little icy shiver pass over her flesh as the door creaked to a close behind her.

'Would you like to be alone for a while?' Angus asked.

'*No!*' Amy said, quickly swinging around to face him. 'Er…I mean it's fine…you know… you being here. It's fine…really…' *Please, don't go,* she added silently.

He didn't answer but she could feel the penetration of his dark contemplative gaze even when she turned her back to look around the room.

Her cousin's narrow bed had been made, its smooth neat cover seeming rather incongruous to Amy, considering Lindsay had never been known for tidiness. For most of Amy's childhood and adolescence she had heard her aunt lamenting the fact that her daughter seemed incapable of keeping order either on her person or with any of her possessions. On the few occasions she had visited her cousin's inner-city flat, Amy had privately wondered how anyone could live in such squalor. Empty take-away food containers and unwashed dishes had seemed to line every surface, along with paint tins and tubes and brushes in amongst her cousin's half-finished artwork. When she had offered to help her tidy up, Lindsay had become extremely agitated until Amy had assured her she wouldn't touch a thing.

Amy went to the bed and, reaching out a hand, ran it down the cover. 'Is this where she was found?' Her voice sounded thin in the silence.

'Yes.'

She turned to look at him, her voice wobbling slightly over the words. 'S-someone must have made her bed.'

'Yes.'

A small sigh escaped her lips. 'I don't think she knew how to do it…' A bubble of emotion popped up from deep inside her and she tried to swallow it back down. 'She was the messiest person I've ever met… She didn't even brush her hair or her teeth unless someone reminded her…'

Amy would have been able to control the second bubble if it hadn't been for Fergus. He padded across from his master's side and gently nudged her hand with his long snout, a soft crooning sound coming from deep inside his throat. She gulped back a sob but another one came to take its place. She rummaged for a tissue but before she could locate one Angus stepped forward and offered her his handkerchief.

She met his gaze through tear-washed eyes as she took the folded square, the brief brush of his fingers yet again jolting her with a charge of his body's heat and energy.

'I'm sorry…' she began in embarrassment. 'I thought I had dealt with all this six months ago.'

He took one of her hands in the dry warmth of his, the slightly roughened pads of his fingers alerting her all over again to his essential maleness. 'You should let it out,' he said. 'It won't do any good buried deep inside.'

She eased her hand out of his and, wiping her eyes, gave him a somewhat twisted smile. 'Doctors aren't supposed to cry, or at least not in front of people.'

'Is that what they teach you in medical school?' he asked.

'No not really,' she said. 'Things have changed from the old days. We're allowed to be human as long as it doesn't affect clinical judgement.'

'Lindsay was your cousin, not your patient,' he reminded her.

'Yes…' Amy said, absently fondling the dog's ears.

'He likes you,' Angus said into the long silence.

She raised her eyes back to his. 'I like him, too,' she said softly.

Three beats of silence passed.

'He looks mean but he's a real softie when you get to know him,' he said.

Amy wondered if he was talking about the dog or obliquely referring to himself. She hunted his face, her eyes still locked on his as the air around them tightened with the tension of their mutual unwilling attraction. She could see it in his eyes, the flicker of male interest as his gaze dipped to her mouth and lingered there. Her tongue came out before she could control it and added a glisten of moisture to the dusty dryness of her lips. The silence was like a throb in the air. A resonant, heavy throb she could feel deep and low in every secret place in her body.

Thump, thump, thump.

She could see the very same pulse beating in his neck, the tanned skin of his throat a temptation she could barely withstand. She could almost taste the salt of his skin in her mouth, her tongue coming out again to sweep across the sensitive surface of her lips.

He suddenly took a step backwards. 'We should get going,' he said in a brusque tone. 'I'll leave you to have a final look around. I'll wait for you outside.'

Amy did her best to ignore the sharp prick of disappointment that deflated her feminine ego to an all-time low. She gave herself a mental kick for being so stupid as to even think he was attracted to her. It was clear he wasn't. She'd been fooling herself, no doubt in an effort to restore her confidence when it came to men.

'At least his dog likes me,' she muttered under her breath, as she took a last look around.

She didn't stay long. She was conscious of the lengthening shadows that seemed all the more menacing now that she was alone. The room felt cold, too, as if a cold sea breeze had found its way beneath the door, curling around her ankles and moving up her body until she began to shiver.

'Why did you do it, Lindsay?' she asked the empty room in a soft whisper. 'Why on earth did you do it?'

There was no answer but the rough unstained floorboards creaked almost painfully as Amy made her way across them to leave…

Angus threw a stick for Fergus with such force it took the dog a few minutes to locate it. He came back with it in his mouth, dropped it at Angus's feet and barked.

'Quiet, Fergus,' Angus said, frowning.

The dog looked instantly crestfallen, his tail stopped wagging and he lowered himself to the ground.

Angus let out a sigh and bent down to ruffle the dog's ears. 'Sorry, boy,' he said gruffly. 'I'm taking it out on you, aren't I?'

He straightened when he heard the sound of Amy approaching, his groin tightening all over again at the sight of her. She had a youthful, totally feminine freshness about her that was a heady reminder of what he had denied himself for too long. It had been so long ago he couldn't quite remember the last time he had held a woman in his arms or even who it had been. But getting involved with the visiting doctor was asking for the sort of trouble he could do without just now. Dr Amy Tanner had suspicion written all over her beautiful face. Why else had she come all this way if not to ask questions he didn't want asked?

'All done?' he asked her, as she came towards him.

She nodded and, releasing a sigh, cast her gaze towards the far end of the beach where the crumbling cliff met the ocean. 'Is that where the caves are?' she asked.

'Yes, but it's not advisable to go too close,' he said. 'The rockface is a bit unstable after recent rain.' He opened the car for her and added, 'I'll go and lock up. Won't be a minute.'

She watched in the side mirror as he returned and put the dog in the back, the warm affection he held for Fergus clearly evident in the way his dark brown eyes softened as he stroked the dog's ears before he closed the door.

Careful, Amy warned herself sternly. Yes, he may be seriously gorgeous and he loves dogs, but he's still a cop.

She turned to face him as he slid in behind the wheel. 'Thank you for bringing me out here,' she said. 'I'm not sure I would have coped very well on my own.'

He gunned the engine and began to back out of the rough driveway, his outstretched arm along the seat close to the back of her neck. 'How long have you had arachnophobia?' he asked.

She bit her lip and looked down at her hands. 'For as long as I can remember.'

Angus swung his gaze her way, his brief look taking in the vulnerable downward turn of her mouth and the slightly hunched set of her slim shoulders. He turned his attention back to the ridged road but he couldn't help wondering what had started that irrational pattern of fear. He knew from experience that a traumatic episode was often cited in the onset of post-traumatic syndrome and a phobia was more or less an extension of that.

'I suppose you think it's totally pathetic that a woman of twenty-seven and a doctor to boot should be scared of spiders,' she said after another moment or two of silence.

'As far as I recall, I didn't express that view.'

'You didn't have to. I could see it on your face yesterday at the hotel.'

'I was momentarily surprised, that's all.'

'You were laughing at me.'

'I can assure you I was not.'

'I think I should warn you that if you have any intention of spreading the news of my phobia around town, I will be very angry with you,' she said.

'Your secret is safe with me.'

She gave a little snort that he took to be disbelief. 'It will ruin my credibility if it got out. I've worked hard to keep it under control.'

'Which clearly hasn't worked.'

'Is that a criticism?'

'No, it was an observation,' he answered.

'But you still think it's pathetic, don't you?'

'I think it's a shame you are controlled by an irrational fear but, no, I don't think it's pathetic. Lots of people have phobias.'

'You're just saying that.'

He blew out a breath of frustration. 'All right, have it your way. I think it's pathetic. Happy now? Is that what you wanted me to say?'

Amy could feel herself backing down. 'I'm sorry,' she mumbled. 'I'm just a little sensitive about it. I don't like people to know how weak I am.'

'It's not a weakness to confront your fears,' he said. 'You've just spent fifteen minutes in a spider-infested environment. That's not weakness—that's courage.'

Amy was surprised at how much his compliment affected her. His comment was so far removed from those of her father's she was tempted to tell him so, but before she could get the words out his radio started to crackle and a voice sounded out from the dashboard, informing Angus of an accident on a back road.

'The volunteer ambulance is about thirty

minutes away,' the voice said. 'Dr Peddington is not answering his phone or pager but the clinic nurse said you had the new doctor with you—is that correct?'

'Yes, that's right,' Angus said taking the next turn. 'We'll be there in ten minutes, tops.'

Amy looked at him after he'd signed off. 'Have we got time to pick up my doctor's bag?'

He gave a quick nod. 'We have to go back through town anyway.'

'What happened, do you know?' she asked in an effort to prepare herself as they approached town a few minutes later.

'One of the locals has rolled his car evidently,' he said. 'That back road is notorious for loose gravel. It sounds nasty, from what Nick Winters was saying.' He sent her a quick glance before adding, 'Have you had any experience with roadside trauma recovery?'

Amy felt herself bristling all over again. What did he think she was, some sort of novice? 'I have both the Australian EMST and UK equivalent trauma qualifications,' she said.

'Just checking,' he said as he pulled up in front of the hotel. 'Is your bag in your car or upstairs?'

'Upstairs,' she said, and jumped out. 'I'll be as quick as I can.'

Angus watched her bolt inside, his fingers drumming against the steering-wheel impatiently. He would have preferred Allan Peddington on a callout like this. Allan was rock steady in a crisis, always in control, which had a calming affect on everyone else around him. Amy Tanner, with her wild curly chestnut hair, pouting mouth and coltish figure, looked like she'd just finished high school. It didn't seem possible she could handle serious trauma and certainly not on a dusty roadside.

She came bounding back with her bag and tossed it on the back seat before getting back in beside him. 'Right. Let's go.'

He drove out of town and took a turn down a back road that led them to the wreckage of an old-model Holden lying on its roof. A man was standing next to a body lying on the side of the road about twenty metres from the car.

'Thank God you're here!' the white-faced man said as he came towards them. 'Is the ambulance on its way?'

'Should be here in ten to fifteen minutes, Nick,'

Angus said as he retrieved Amy's bag for her and carried it towards the victim.

'It's young Bobby Williams,' Nick informed Angus soberly. 'He's in a bad way.'

Amy began to examine the injured man. 'He's unconscious and not responding to pain or voice,' she said, more to herself than to anyone else in an effort to maintain professional calm. She knew this was going to test her skills. She had limited experience with roadside retrieval and, as the man called Nick had said, the victim looked as if he was seriously injured. She could feel the adrenalin surging through her system and had to fight to control the slight tremble of her hands.

'His left femur is at an angle and obviously fractured, and he has abrasions all over the front of his chest where he's slid along the gravel.' She took a breath to steady herself and asked Angus, 'Can you help me to steady his neck? His airway's obstructed—I'll need to clear it.'

Amy donned gloves and goggles and began removing debris from the boy's mouth. Without instruction Angus held the head steady while she tried chin lift and jaw thrust, but there was no air movement. A Guedell's airway did not improve the situation.

'I'm going to have to intubate him,' she said, suppressing another wave of panic.

Angus moved around to the victim's side, and with a gloved hand on each side expertly stabilised the boy's neck while Amy retrieved the laryngoscope and an endotracheal tube from the kit. It was a bit of a struggle because of blood in the back of the throat, which Amy had no means to aspirate, but somehow she managed to intubate him regardless. While she tied in the tube and started bagging on air using the Air-Viva set from her kit, Angus automatically sized and fitted a hard cervical collar. Once fitted, this allowed him to take over ventilation while Amy continued assessment.

'You seem to know what you're doing,' she remarked as she put her stethoscope to the victim's chest to check breathing. 'You must have done this before as well.'

'Once or twice too often,' Angus confessed with a grim set to his features. God, he hated accidents like this. He felt so useless and out of control. He had to force his mind away from that day with Dan.

That day with Dan.

He gave an inward grimace. It sounded like the title of a movie, not the life of his best mate draining away beneath his hands…

'There's no air entry on the right side,' Amy said, and, feeling the trachea, added, 'The trachea's shifted to the left.' She percussed the chest to find it was dull on the right side and even more so on the left.

'The neck veins were distended when I put on the cervical collar,' Angus said, forcing the images of Dan's grief-stricken wife and children out of his head.

'I'm pretty sure he's got a right pneumothorax but the chest isn't that resonant,' Amy said. 'It could be a haemothorax. If we put in a chest drain without IV access, we could kill him with blood loss.'

'He's very difficult to ventilate,' Angus said, as a vision of the Bobby's parents slipped into his mind. His stomach clenched with dread as he added, 'If we don't do something soon, he's going to die anyway.'

Amy took a 12-gauge canula and, after swabbing the skin with alcohol, inserted it into the right second intercostal space. A small amount of air and a trickle of blood came out. 'It's definitely not a tension pneumothorax,' she said. 'I think he's bled into the right chest. He needs a chest drain and IV resus.' She looked up in rising panic. 'When is that ambulance coming?'

'Shouldn't be too long now,' Angus said with enviable calm. 'Can you get an IV line in?'

'Yes, I've got a couple of bags of saline—that might tide him over for a short period,' she added, taking the pulse and fitting a BP cuff. 'Pulse is 140 and BP is only 80 systolic.'

She inserted a 14-gauge canula, but with a lot of difficulty as the victim's veins were not distending with the tourniquet. She started a saline bag running full bore, and then got another line into the other arm and started the second bag of saline.

The wail of the ambulance sounded in the distance and Amy exchanged a brief glance of relief with Angus. She took over ventilation and asked him to straighten the patient's leg but there was no pain response. Amy noted the patient's GCS at 8 or 9.

The ambulance arrived but the two volunteers were clearly not very experienced. Amy felt her heart sink when she saw the way they hovered about, waiting for direction.

'Right,' she said, pointing to the woman in her mid-fifties who had introduced herself as Joan. 'Can you get me a chest drain set from the ambulance?'

Jim, the other, elderly ambo, set about procuring a Donway splint from one of the ambulance cupboards.

Amy was able to insert a right chest drain without local anesthesia. About 200 ml of blood immediately drained out into the underwater bottle, then nothing else. She joined up a litre of colloid to each IV line and asked Angus, 'Are the neck veins still distended?'

Angus loosened the collar and answered, 'Yes, more than before.'

She listened to the heart with the stethoscope but the heart sounded very muffled and hard to hear.

Jim by this stage had fitted and pumped up the Donway, and now set about connecting an ECG, while Joan rechecked the victim's obs.

'BP 70 systolic, Dr Tanner, pulse 140,' she reported.

'Thanks, Joan.' Amy sat back on her heels

and looked at Angus, not even bothering to disguise her fear. 'I think he has a haemopericardium. That would make sense from the mechanism of injury—a sudden deceleration as he was thrown out of the car. The standard thing to do is put in a pericardial needle. I've never done that before, and the reports say it might not be that effective anyway. And it could kill him if I puncture his heart or a coronary vessel.'

'Looks to me like he's running out of chances anyway,' Angus said. 'Even if we do manage to stabilise him, he still has a long journey ahead of him to Geraldton. I've called for the flying doctor on the police radio but they couldn't give me an accurate ETA. They're in the air north of Geraldton now on a routine transfer. They're turning back and deciding whether they have to drop off their transfer patient first. I've told them how urgent things here are.'

Amy gave him a grim look and reached for a long needle and attached a three-way tap and syringe. Swabbing the upper abdomen with alcohol, she inserted the needle just to the left of the xiphisternum, aiming for the tip of the left scapula.

'The ECG's showing funny rhythms, Dr Tanner,' Jim informed her.

Amy looked at the monitor and saw the runs of VF. 'Crunch time,' she said, and further advanced the needle, aspirating as she went. Suddenly she was able to withdraw dark blood and, using the three-way tap, took out 40 ml more blood.

'BP's come up to 110 systolic—something seems to be working,' Jim said.

Angus responded to a call coming in on his phone. Then he clipped it back on his belt. 'The plane is landing in ten minutes, they've kept their transfer patient on board. We'll meet them at the airstrip. They'll take him straight down to Geraldton. But you'd better go with him. This guy's not out of the woods yet.'

'But—'

'I'll organise someone to bring you back to Marraburra,' he said.

'Thanks,' she said, and supervised the loading of the accident victim into the back of the ambulance. She suppressed an inward sigh and gathered up her things in preparation for the journey, deciding that this probably wasn't the best time to tell Sergeant Angus Ford that, along with spiders, she wasn't too keen on small aircraft either.

CHAPTER SEVEN

AMY was totally exhausted by the time the patient had been assessed by the Geraldton A and E team. She had been convinced for the entire journey that at any minute the plane would come crashing down. To her shame she'd even had to use a sick bag a couple of times when they'd hit a patch of turbulence. In her misery she had begun to mentally compose the next day's newspaper headlines: YOUNG FEMALE GP KILLED IN MERCY DASH WITH ACCIDENT VICTIM.

She brought her head up when she realised someone was speaking to her in A and E.

'You did a great job,' Derek Payton, the A and E doctor on duty, said as the patient was being transferred to the operating Theatre. 'I heard it's only your second day on the coast.'

'Yes,' she said with a tired smile. 'And here I was thinking things would be pretty quiet way out here.'

'Yeah, well, not always,' he said. 'Is someone coming to pick you up?'

'The local sergeant was organising a lift for me.'

'Help yourself to coffee and a sandwich in the doctors' room on the third floor while you wait.' He looked at his watch and added, 'You've been here almost three hours so it shouldn't be much longer. I'll give you a buzz when your lift arrives.'

'Thanks,' she said and made her way to the elevator.

The doctors' room was thankfully vacant, which meant Amy could sink into one of the armchairs, kick off her shoes, lay her head back and close her eyes. She was way beyond appetite and although the aroma of coffee in the air was tempting, she felt too tired to get up and pour herself a cup.

She woke what felt like only seconds later when someone touched her on the arm. She blinked and Angus's handsome features came into focus. She rubbed at her gritty eyes and dragged herself upright from her slumped position, her cheeks feeling warm all of a sudden.

'I must have fallen asleep,' she said as she got to her feet and straightened her crumpled clothes.

'You probably needed it,' he said. 'Are you ready to leave?'

She met his eyes with a questioning look. 'I thought you were organising someone to pick me up?'

'I did—me.'

She gnawed at her bottom lip as she began to hunt for her missing shoe.

'Is this what you're looking for?' He held out her shoe.

'Yes…' She took it from him and stuffed her foot back into it. 'But I could have waited till morning. You didn't have to drive all the way down here just for me.'

'I had to bring Bobby's parents down in any case,' he said. 'His father is in a wheelchair and his mother isn't a confident driver. Besides they were both pretty upset about their son's accident, especially as alcohol was involved.'

'All the same, you must be tired,' she said, trying to squash her disappointment that he hadn't made the trip just for her after all. 'It seems a month since Matt Healy's shoulder and yet it was only hours ago.'

'I'm used to long hours,' he said, and shouldered open the door. 'Come on. You can have another power nap in the car.'

Amy determined she would stay awake for the whole journey but somehow as soon as they were on their way her eyelids began to drop as if weighted with house bricks and her head began to slip sideways…

She woke as the car came to halt outside the hotel. The lights were all off and the place looked deserted and even more rundown without the glare of fluorescent illumination.

'Have you got a key to the side entrance?' Angus asked.

'Um…' She bit her lip when she realised it was on her car keyring, which was upstairs in her room. 'Not on me right now.'

He gave her a musing look. 'I don't quite fancy waking Bill Huxley at this hour. Perhaps you'd better come home with me for what's left of the night.'

'Do you really think that's necessary?' she asked. 'I mean, surely Bill won't mind opening the door for me just this once.'

'You can take your chances with Bill, who probably sank a few after closing time and is now sleeping them off, or you can take a chance on me. Take it or leave it. But to reassure you, I'm sober as a judge and dog tired so if you're anticipating any trouble from me, forget it.'

'I wasn't for a moment implying that you—'

'Yes, you were,' he interjected. 'You keep looking at me as if I'm going to drag you off to my cave and ravish you.'

'I do not!'

'Yes, you do,' he said, 'which makes me wonder what type of guys you've been hanging out with in London.'

'No one like you, I can assure you,' she tossed back.

'I kind of assumed that,' he returned.

She glared at him. 'What do you mean by that?'

He ignored her question by asking one of his own. 'So what's it to be, Dr Tanner? Catching a couple of hours on the steps of the Dolphin View or a comfortable bed at my place?'

'Well…' She sent him a sheepish look. 'When you put it like *that*…'

His lips moved upwards in what could almost be described as a smile as he put the car back into gear. 'My place it is.'

* * *

Unlike the hotel they had just left, his house was all the more attractive in the soft glow of moonlight. The blue-black blanket of stars above combined with the soporific pulse of the ocean crawling below made Amy wish she hadn't been so adamant about her choice of accommodation. The thought of a bathroom all to herself and a bed that didn't squeak was suddenly all too tempting.

And no spiders!

Angus led her inside where Fergus greeted her like an old friend, the soft whimper he gave her as he nudged her hand thrilling her that he had accepted her so readily.

'Cool it, Fergus,' Angus scolded. 'You're making a fool of yourself.'

'No, he's not,' Amy insisted. 'Besides, don't you know women love a man who's prepared to wear his heart on his sleeve?'

'Not any of the women I know,' he said as he tossed his keys to the counter before removing his gun and phone from his belt and laying them beside them.

Amy tilted her head at him. 'So how many women do you actually know, Sergeant Ford?'

He unclipped his pager and laid it next to his gun, his eyes steady on hers. 'Are you by any chance flirting with me, Dr Tanner?' he asked.

'No, of course not!'

He raised his brows at her vehement denial, the line of his mouth faintly mocking.

'Please, don't concern yourself,' she said, folding her arms. 'You're *so* not my type.'

'I brought you here to offer you a bed, not a relationship,' he said. 'However, if you're looking for someone to entertain you while you're in town, I'm sure I could summon up the enthusiasm to do so.'

She sent him a flinty look. 'I'm perfectly happy at the hotel and I am definitely *not* looking for a relationship, and certainly not a temporary one and definitely not with you.'

'Every unattached woman is looking for a relationship.'

'Not this one,' she said, turning up her nose. 'I'm still getting over the last one.'

'How long ago was that?'

'Eighteen months.'

'Time to get back on the horse, so to speak.'

She tightened her mouth without responding.

'So what happened?' he asked as he led the way to the kitchen.

Amy followed and at his invitation pulled out a breakfast bar stool to sit on. 'To this day I'm not really sure…'

Angus turned to look at her, noting her small frown and the cute way her teeth sank into the fullness of her bottom lip. 'It's like that sometimes,' he offered, thinking of his own relationship disasters.

She released her lip and he watched as the tip of her tongue came out and smoothed over the small indentation her teeth had made.

'I guess I read the signals all wrong or something,' she said. 'You know…saw things that weren't there in an effort to reassure myself things were on track.'

'He was a doctor?'

'Yes, an anaesthetist. He's married with a baby now.'

'Ouch.'

Amy felt a rueful smile tug at her mouth. 'Very definitely ouch.'

He pushed himself away from the bench to open

the fridge. 'Do you want a cold drink? Orange juice or milk?' he asked over his shoulder.

'Um…no, thanks,' she answered, trying not to stare at his firm buttocks as he leaned into the fridge.

He took out a carton of milk and, closing the door of the fridge, leaned his hips back against the nearest bench and drained the contents.

Amy felt a fluttery pulse inside her stomach when he lowered the empty carton to the bench. 'Er…' She tapped her finger against her upper lip. 'You have a milk moustache.'

He wiped his mouth with the back of his hand. 'Gone?'

'All gone,' she said, and blushed like a schoolgirl.

He held her gaze for a tiny beat before he pushed himself away from the bench. 'Come on, I'll show you to your room.'

Amy followed him on legs that weren't quite steady, mentally chiding herself for being so foolish as to be affected by such an everyday thing as a man drinking out of a milk carton. *Sheesh!* She had to get some control. What on earth would her mother say if she told her she was attracted to a cop?

She was concentrating so hard on putting one foot in front of the other she didn't realise Angus had stopped halfway down the hall. She cannoned into him as he turned, his hands going to her upper arms to steady her.

'Whoa there,' he said, still holding her.

'Oops... I mean sorry. I didn't realise you'd stopped.'

His mouth tilted in a half smile. 'For a moment there I thought you were going to fall flat on your face, like this morning,' he said.

Actually, I think I'm falling in love, Amy surprised herself by admitting silently. She held her breath, not game to draw in a new one with his chest so close to hers. 'Um...you can let me go now,' she managed to croak out, her colour still high.

His hands loosened their grip and gradually fell away to drop by his sides. 'There's a bathrobe on the back of the door and fresh towels in the main bathroom two doors down,' he said, his voice sounding faintly rusty.

'Thank you...'

'What time do you need to be at the clinic in the morning?'

'Eight-thirty or so.'

'Fine,' he said. 'I'll run you in.'

'Um…you don't happen to have a spare tooth-brush, do you?' she asked. Pausing for a moment, she found herself confessing, 'I was sick in the plane.'

He stood looking at her.

'What's that look for?' she asked, starting to squirm under his scrutiny. 'Lot's of people get airsick.'

He shook his head at her and moved past. 'There's a spare toothbrush in the cupboard beneath the basin. Goodnight.'

Amy spun around to glare at him as he strode away to his room. 'Lots and lots of people,' she reiterated. 'I bet even *you* would be sick, given the right circumstances.'

'Goodnight, Dr Tanner,' he said in a bored tone.

'Goodnight, Sergeant Ford,' she said crisply. 'And just in case you're interested, I was only sick twice. Believe me, that's sort of a record. I'm usually much worse.'

He didn't answer but she was sure he was still rolling his eyes as he disappeared into his bedroom.

* * *

Amy woke during the next hour or so to hear a soft scratching noise outside her door. Her eyes sprang open and she stiffened in the bed as she imagined a giant spider trying to make its way under the door. She began to talk herself through the panic, taking deep breaths as she reached for the bedside lamp, the soft glow instantly calming her fears as the scratching sound this time was accompanied by a low-pitched doggy whine.

She tossed the covers aside and, picking up the towel she'd used earlier after her quick but totally refreshing shower, she covered her nakedness and opened the door. 'Fergus,' she said, looking down at the soulful brown eyes gazing up at her. 'What's wrong? Can't you sleep?'

The dog gave another whine and began moving down the hall, stopping now and again to look back at her as if to ask her to follow him.

'Hey, boy,' she whispered as she tiptoed past Angus's room. 'Do you need to go outside? Is that what's wrong?'

The dog finally came to a stop in front of the front door and gave another whine deep in his throat.

'OK, I'll let you out, but don't be long,' she said

as she opened the door. 'I really need my beauty sleep and I'm about five hours short as it is.'

Fergus slunk off to the side of the house, the soft pad of his paws drowned out by the pounding of the surf below. Amy lifted her face to look at the brilliant night sky, her nostrils flaring to take in the fresh salty air.

A bird shuffled in a nearby shrub, its soft chirping signalling that dawn wasn't far away.

Amy stepped away from the open door to inspect the eastern sky, which the bulk of the house hid from view. The first light of the sun was streaking the sky with fingers of gold that were stretching outwards and upwards as if to collect all the shining stars and keep them hidden until the next night.

There was a soft thud behind her and she spun around to find the front door had closed on a breath of a breeze. She made her way back to the door, her heart sinking when she discovered it had locked on closing.

'Typical security-conscious cop,' she muttered under her breath as she jiggled the doorknob, to no avail.

She blew out a breath of frustration and, clutching her slipping towel, whispered to Fergus. 'Here, boy, come on. I want you with me when I wake up your master. He's not going to be happy to be woken after less than two hours' sleep.'

Fergus was nowhere to be seen or heard. Amy strained her ears for the sound of his paws on the gravelly area in front of the house but it was as quiet as the grave.

She called out again, slightly louder this time, but her voice came back to her in a ghostly echo that lifted the skin on her bare arms.

'And here I was thinking you were well trained,' she grumbled softly as she stepped gingerly over the rough gravel in her bare feet, one hand clutching her towel to her breasts. 'Come on, Fergus, you big mutt. Get your backside inside or I'll tell your master what a wicked truant you really are. Some police dog you turned out to be. You can't even obey the simplest orders.'

She rounded another corner of the house and opened her mouth to call out again when a tall dark figure stepped out of the shadows of the shrubbery on her right. Fear choked back her scream as every other survival instinct came to the fore. She fought viciously against the hands reaching for her, kicking and wriggling until she landed on the gravel on her back with her assailant on top of her. She bucked and arched in spite of the rough stones digging into her back and shoulders. In fact, if she hadn't been so absolutely terrified she would have even been a little proud of herself, given she'd never progressed past a white belt in tae kwon do.

Somehow she managed to open her mouth beneath the pressure of the palm against her and sank her teeth into it, but all it produced in her assailant was a cut-off expletive.

She wasn't quite sure how she did it but somehow she managed to catch him off guard and land a hard punch to his face before she rolled away, but it cost her the covering of the towel. She scrambled to her feet and began to run, shrieking at the top of her voice, 'Fergus! Angus! *Help!*'

She had only taken three stumbling steps when Angus's deep voice halted her. 'It's all right. It's me.'

She swung around to glare at him, her chest still heaving in fear. *'You!'*

He stepped out of the shadows and in the

spreading light of dawn she saw his eyebrow wound had split open and was bleeding again.

She crossed her arms over her chest. 'Would you, please, hand me my towel?' she bit out in between ragged breaths as her heart rate struggled to return to normal.

'What were you doing outside, for God's sake?' he asked with a heavy frown. 'I could have hurt you.'

She lifted her chin at him. 'You *did* hurt me.' She gave him an icy glare. 'My back and shoulders are rubbed raw. What the hell were you doing? Why didn't you call out, instead of jumping on me and throwing me to the ground like that?'

'I thought you were an intruder and I did *not* throw you to the ground,' he said, a thin thread of anger entering his tone as he wiped the blood away from his face. 'You were struggling like a wildcat and took us both down.'

Amy would have put her hands on her hips but she needed them to offer what little modesty she could achieve in the brightening light of the morning. 'Will you, *please,* hand me my towel?' she asked again.

He turned around and, finding the towel, scooped it up off the ground and handed it to her without a word.

Amy took it with one hand, her breath tripping in her chest when she saw the way his eyes moved lazily over her. 'Do you mind?' She flashed her eyes at him in indignation.

His eyes came back to hers but not before he had seen practically all there was to see, she noted with burning resentment.

'You didn't answer my question,' he said. 'What were you doing outside?'

She secured the towel and, sending him another reproachful glare, informed him coldly, 'It was Fergus's fault. He woke me and begged to be let out. The door swung shut behind me.'

'Has he come back?'

'How would I know?' she asked. 'I've been too busy fighting off my would-be assailant.'

'Sorry about that,' he said. 'I thought I heard voices. I came outside to check.'

'I was talking to Fergus. That's probably what you heard.'

'I thought it was a male voice.'

'Oh…'

'You'd better go inside and clean up,' he said leading the way back to the door and unlocking it for her. 'I'll just do a quick check of the boatshed and see where Fergus has got to.'

'Your head looks like it needs to be re-stitched,' she said as the light from the house shone on his face. She bit her lip and mumbled self-consciously, 'I didn't mean to hit you that hard. Sorry.'

'Who taught you how to punch like that?' he asked with a twisted smile.

'Believe me, you really wouldn't want to know,' she said, and disappeared inside.

CHAPTER EIGHT

ANGUS searched the property before taking the cliff path to the beach, but if anyone had been there they had moved on. He looked out to sea and saw the faint light of a fishing boat in the distance but the vessel was too far away to have been responsible for the voices he'd heard, even though, at this time of day, sound carried over the water.

He met Fergus as he turned back for the path. The dog's coat was sandy and damp, as if he had been in the sea.

'You picked a bad time for a swim, mate,' he said, reaching to tickle his ears. 'You're supposed to be keeping an eye on things around here. You're getting soft, old boy. One pretty face and trim figure and you go to pieces.'

Fergus licked his hand and whined softly.

'Yeah, right,' Angus said wryly, heading back towards the house. 'Believe me, mate, I'm trying to take my own advice. I'm really trying, but she's quite a package even if she does have a lead foot.'

He heard Amy in the bathroom on his way past. He stopped and gave the door a gentle knock. 'You all right in there?'

The door swung open to reveal her dressed in a bathrobe. 'Look at my back!' she railed at him, swinging round and lowering the robe to show him her back and shoulders. 'I look like I've been dragged across a bed of nails.'

Angus couldn't help wincing in empathy. Her soft skin was pockmarked with gravel rash, some spots dark where the tiny stones had dug in and stayed put.

'I'll get some tweezers and get that gravel out for you,' he offered.

She pulled the bathrobe back up and turned back to face him as she tied it securely. 'I'd better do your head first,' she said. 'It's still seeping blood.'

He took a facecloth from the rack and pressed it to the wound above his eye, grimacing when he removed it and saw the red stain. 'It'll be fine in a minute.'

She blew out a breath of frustration. 'You can quit

it with that I'm-a-bulletproof-macho-man routine,'
she said. 'Your eyebrow needs re-stitching otherwise it won't heal the way it should, and then no
doubt I'll get the blame for scarring you for life.'

Brown eyes challenged blue for several
pulsing seconds.

'All right,' he said. 'You go first.'

'I'll get my bag,' she said, and brushed past him.

She came back a short time later with her bag
and set it on the bench that housed the basin.

'You're probably going to have a real shiner
by morning,' she said as she bathed the area
with betadine.

'I hate to point it out, but it *is* morning.'

Amy felt the rumble of his deep voice as she
brushed closer to place the first suture, and her
hand wobbled. 'Keep still,' she said.

'I didn't move a muscle.'

'Stop talking, then,' she said. 'I can't concentrate.'

'If you can't concentrate, maybe I should get
Allan Peddington to do it.'

'Shut up and let me get on with it.'

'You were much quicker last time,' he said.

'I've been awake most of the night and I've

been attacked and rolled like a rug across a gravel path, so if I'm a little bit off par, don't blame me.'

'If you had woken me when Fergus came to your door, none of this would have happened,' he said as she put in the final stitch.

'So it's all my fault now, is it?' she asked, stripping off her gloves and tossing them in the bin. 'Your dog came to me and I assumed it would be all right to let him out. Besides, you'd had a long drive. I was trying to be helpful, if you must know, but apparently you don't agree.'

He got to his feet which made the bathroom seem way too small. 'Turn around,' he commanded.

She almost put her neck out, looking up at him. 'Maybe I'll let Allan Peddington fix me. At least he'll know what he's doing.'

A tiny nerve flickered at the side of his mouth. 'Turn around, Dr Tanner.'

Amy felt her tummy give a tiny tremor of excitement at the brooding dark intensity in his eyes as they held hers. 'No,' she said.

His hands came down on her shoulders and turned her so swiftly her breath came out in a startled whoosh. He was standing so close she could feel the brace of his thighs behind her, their steely presence sending her heart on a roller-coaster ride.

'Pull the bathrobe down or I'll do it for you,' he said.

After a moment's hesitation she wriggled it down past her shoulders and muttered, 'No wonder you're not married or attached. No woman would ever put up with your caveman attitude.'

'I'm not married or attached because I don't have time for female histrionics,' he returned as he began to bathe her upper back with a solution of betadine.

'Ouch!' She winced. 'That hurts!'

'I rest my case,' he drawled.

She gritted her teeth when he started using the tweezers, her hands gripping the edge of the bench in an effort to stop herself from squealing in pain.

I'll show him, she silently fumed. *I'm not going to make a sound.*

'Right,' he said after a few agonising, eye-watering minutes. 'That's the upper back done. Anywhere else?'

Amy decided against telling him her buttocks had taken their fare share of gravel from the path. 'No,' she said as she turned.

His eyes locked down on hers.

The air tightened around them, each second beginning to throb with a current of erotic promise. Amy felt the magnetic pull of his body; his naked chest, so close her fingertips ached to explore his muscular contours to see if they were as hard and sculpted as they looked.

She sent her tongue out to moisten her lips, her stomach free-falling when she saw his eyes darken as they followed the movement. His throat rose and fell on a swallow, as if he was fighting the temptation to close the tiny distance that separated them.

Her eyes went to his mouth, her breath stumbling to a halt as she saw the way its normally hard contours softened slightly as he came closer, his warm breath caressing her upturned face as his eyelashes fanned down over his eyes.

He paused just above her parted lips, as if he was still struggling with himself, but before he could change his mind, Amy closed the space between them and sealed his mouth with the full softness of hers.

It was like an explosion.

Flames of need flashed and sparked as their

mouths fused, the white-hot scorch of hard male on soft female lips, the burning stroke and glide of tongues duelling as the kiss drifted into even more dangerous sensual territory.

Amy whimpered in delight when he took over the kiss with a commanding force that was somewhere between pleasure and pain. The bruising quality of his mouth grinding against hers spoke of physical needs left unmet for far too long. There was anger in his kiss, anger and frustration and red-hot desire. She felt it ridge his lower body as his blood surged through his veins, the thickness of him against her sending her senses spinning.

His tongue probed and thrust against hers, calling it into a dance of heated sexual purpose. Excitement zinged along her nerve endings, her skin tightening all over in anticipation of his touch on other parts of her body. Her belly quivered and shook with desire, her inner thighs already anointed with the dewy moistness of her arousal. Her breasts swelled and ached, their hardened points rubbing up against him as he crushed her to him, his mouth still wreaking its sensual havoc on hers.

He dragged his mouth off hers after another

few breathless moments, his eyes glittering with rampant need, his chest rising and falling as he fought to regain control. 'Now, that was a really stupid thing to for you to do,' he said.

Her eyes widened in affront. 'What did *I* do?'

'You started it by kissing me first.'

'I did not!'

'Yes, you did,' he said. 'I admit I was tempted, but I wasn't going to go through with it.'

'Oh really?' Her expression was sceptical.

He held her challenging look with ease. 'I'm as human as the next man,' he said. 'When a woman throws herself at me, like you did, it takes a moment or two to tame the instinctive response.'

'I did *not* throw myself at you!'

'Don't get me wrong, Dr Tanner. You're a good-looking woman but anything that happens between us is not going to work out in the long term.'

She gave him a scathing look. 'If you think for one moment I'd be interested in any length of term with someone like you then you've got yourself an even bigger ego problem than I originally thought. You're exactly the sort of man I have avoided all my dating life.'

'Good to know where we both stand on this,'

he said. 'I didn't want you to get the wrong idea about one kiss.'

She scooped up her doctor's bag and stormed out of the bathroom with her head held high. 'It wasn't such a great kiss anyway,' she tossed over her shoulder.

Angus didn't answer but when he turned and caught sight of himself in the mirror he found his fingers had somehow crept up to his mouth where the softness of hers had pressed against his…

Amy sat in a stiff silence as Angus drove her to town an hour or so later. She felt his gaze swing in her direction once or twice but stalwartly refused to acknowledge it. She hated that he had painted her as some sort of female desperado in search of a temporary mate. Her skin still prickled with irritation at his summation of her character. Who was he to cast the first stone anyway? He was locked out here in the wilderness with nothing but a dog for company on the long lonely nights. At least she had tried to have some sort of life with Simon, even if it hadn't worked out the way she had hoped.

She mumbled a quick thanks as he pulled up

outside the hotel so she could get changed before starting at the clinic.

'I forgot to tell you what a good job you did yesterday with Bobby Williams,' he said through his open window as she began to stalk away. 'I wasn't sure you'd be able to manage such severe injuries.'

She turned back to look at him, a tiny pout hovering around her mouth. 'I hope that wasn't too painful, Sergeant,' she said. 'Giving me a compliment, I mean.'

'I thought I gave you the biggest compliment earlier this morning,' he returned with an unreadable look.

'Oh, yes, indeed you did,' she answered. 'You told me how resistible I am. Thanks a bunch.'

'You should be thankful I didn't take advantage of your…er…generosity,' he said.

Amy came back to stand in front of his window and, leaning down, eyeballed him determinedly. 'I forgot to tell *you* something yesterday,' she said echoing his earlier words.

'Go right ahead,' Angus said, doing his best to keep his eyes trained on hers instead of the tempting shadow of her cleavage currently on show.

'The nicest thing about you is your dog,' she said. 'As far as I can see, it's the only thing you've got going for you.'

His lips twitched. 'Is that so, Dr Tanner? I'm sure he'll be delighted to hear it.'

'And another thing,' she went on, with her blue eyes flashing at him furiously. 'You could have stopped that kiss before it started so it's no good laying the blame solely at my door.'

He gave her a nod of assent. 'Point taken.'

A little frown began to tease her brow. 'So you admit it was just as much your fault?'

'It was just a kiss, Dr Tanner, and like you said—not a particularly good one.' He put the car into gear and gave the engine a couple of revs before adding coolly, 'Have a nice day.'

Amy watched as he drove off, taking her chance of the last word with him. She huffed out a breath of pique and trudged into the hotel.

'Morning, Dr Tanner,' Bill called out from behind the bar. 'I left the side door open for you last night but I see you spent the night with Angus.'

Amy felt her face heating. 'Um…I didn't realise you had left it open,' she said. 'Sergeant Ford told me it would be locked. He thought it best not to wake you. We got back rather late from Geraldton.'

'I heard about young Bobby's accident. He's been asking for that for months, you know. He's got in with the wrong crowd. I hope he makes it, for the sake of his parents if not for himself.'

'He's doing OK, or so the surgeon said when I phoned this morning,' she said. 'He's going to have a long period of rehabilitation but hopefully it will give him time to see the error of his ways.'

'It's a nice place Angus is looking after out there at the Point, isn't it?' Bill said as he gave the bench another wipe.

'Yes…it's very nice.'

He smiled a knowing smile. 'You know you wouldn't be putting my nose out of joint if you moved out there with him. It's not much of a room for you upstairs and sharing a bathroom with the other guests can't be too pleasant, not to mention the dining room, which is probably nothing like those posh London restaurants you're used to.'

'It's fine, really.'

'Yeah, well, I thought I should warn you old Maurie Morrison is back in town,' he said. 'He's a bit of a drifter who blows in and out now and again. He's in room four. I hope he doesn't disturb you. He's a nice enough bloke. A bit lonely since his wife died so if you haven't got time to chat, make sure you let him know. He can talk the leg off an iron pot and he takes ages in the bathroom.'

'I'm sure he won't be any bother to me,' Amy reassured him pleasantly.

'Will you be in for dinner tonight? The kitchen opens at six and closes at seven-thirty. Betty's a bit of a stickler for punctuality but if you're late don't worry. I can always rustle up some left-overs for you.'

Amy tried not to think of her beautifully appointed kitchen in her apartment in Sydney and her massive pile of gourmet cookbooks. 'Leftovers will be fine,' she said.

Bill gave her a grin. 'You have yourself a nice day, now, Dr Tanner.'

She gave him a weak smile. 'I sure will.'

And she would have if it hadn't been for her second-last patient.

Mona Tennant was a woman in her late sixties who obviously didn't require the diagnostic skills of a doctor. She came in with a full list of medications she insisted be prescribed for her without a prior examination or history taken.

'I'm sorry, Mrs Tennant.' Amy tried for the third time to reason with her. 'I can't prescribe narcotic medication for pain unless I know the source of pain. I see from your notes that Dr Ridley ordered a MRI scan of your lower back some months ago. Did you have one taken? I can't see any evidence of the report in your file.'

'Of course I didn't have it done,' the elderly woman said. 'Why would I waste all that time and money travelling all the way to Geraldton for a procedure that will tell me nothing I don't already know? I have a bad back. I've had it for years. Now, if you're not going to give me my pills, I'll go and see Dr Peddington instead.'

'Mrs Tennant, it's not that I don't want to help you but it would make things easier if I knew exactly what it was I was actually treating. Back pain can be debilitating and needs proper management. But sometimes, instead of drugs, some simple exercises or physiotherapy can be just as good if not more effective.'

'Well, forget about the painkillers and write me

up for some nerve pills,' Mrs Tennant said. 'But make them stronger this time. The dosage Dr Ridley gave me last time didn't do a thing.'

Amy glanced back down at the notes. 'But, Mrs Tennant, ten milligrams of Valium is considered a reasonably high dose. Five milligrams is usually enough to settle feelings of anxiety or sleeplessness.'

The old woman pursed her lips for a moment. 'What about the antibiotics, then? I need them in case I get a cold.'

Amy only just resisted the urge to roll her eyes. 'Taking antibiotics when you don't need them can make you resistant to them when you do. Most colds are viral—they only need antibiotics if an infection moves onto the chest or into the nasal passages.'

Mrs Tennant got to her feet and threw Amy a look of disdain. 'Just as well you're only going to be here three months, young lady,' she said. 'Most of us would end up dead and buried if you stayed any longer for lack of proper medical care.'

'Mrs Tennant, I—'

'I know when I need medication. I haven't

been on this earth almost seventy years without learning a thing or two about my own body.'

'I'm sure you're very good at—'

'And another thing,' she huffed and puffed before Amy could finish her sentence. 'Everyone knows why you're really here. You're not interested in the locals at all. All you're interested in is stirring the pot over Lindsay Redgrove's suicide.'

Amy's mouth fell open.

'Don't bother denying it,' the woman went on. 'You were seen with Sergeant Ford out at her shack yesterday at Caveside Cove. The whole town is talking about it.'

'I had a very good reason for wanting to visit Lindsay's shack.'

'Oh, really?' Mrs Tennant looked sceptical. 'Now, what would that be, I wonder?'

'I'm her cousin, that's why.' As soon as Amy had said the words she wished she hadn't.

Mrs Tennant frowned. 'Her cousin? You don't look anything like her in build or looks.'

'No, I know, but that doesn't mean we weren't related. I wanted to visit the place she loved.'

'Then why not be up front about it instead of

going about it so furtively? You won't win any friends out here with such underhand tactics, let me tell you.'

'I didn't and don't see that it's anyone's business but my own.'

The elderly woman peered at her over her glasses. 'If you cared about your cousin, you would have come and visited her before she got so desperate as to take her own her life.'

Amy had to swallow against her rising guilt. 'I was planning to as soon as I finished my term in London.'

'Yes, well, you were too late,' Mrs Tennant said unnecessarily.

'I realise that.'

'I hope you are going to leave her in peace. She did what she did and it should be left at that.'

'I don't want to cause any trouble,' Amy explained. 'I just wanted to pay my respects.'

Mrs Tennant's brows beetled above her bird-like eyes. 'It would have taken less than a day to do that. Why come here for three months?'

It was a good question but Amy wasn't prepared to answer it, or at least not honestly.

'I'm between jobs,' she said instead. 'It seemed a good chance to visit this side of the country.'

'So what do you think of Sergeant Ford?'

Amy was momentarily thrown by the question and looked blankly at the older woman.

'Are you going to move in with him?' Mrs Tennant asked.

'No.'

'You sound rather definite.'

'I am.'

'He needs some company out there.'

'I'm sure he'll find someone.'

'The hotel can't be that comfortable,' Mrs Tennant said. 'Why would you want to stay there when you can stay at the sergeant's place for free?'

'I'm sure it's a lovely spot but—'

'You stayed there last night,' the elderly woman interrupted her. 'Everyone knows you did.'

Amy felt the heat storm into her cheeks again. 'We were late getting back to town. The hotel was locked up and…and Sergeant Ford offered me a place to stay for what was left of the night.'

'So how was it?'

'How was what?'

'Spending the night at his place.'

Amy was feeling as if her doctor status had taken a sudden nose dive. 'It was fine. Now, if you'll excuse me, I have one last patient to see.'

'The Healy boy, right?' Mrs Tennant said with another purse of her lips. 'That mother of his needs a kick up the backside if you ask me. Talk about neurotic. Mind you, the boy's been a bit of a handful but Sergeant Ford has taken him under his wing.'

'Yes, I've heard what a good job he does with the local youth.'

'He's a good man is our sergeant but in need of a good woman,' Mrs Tennant said.

'I'm sure he's more than able to find one for himself,' Amy offered pertly.

'He's got scars, you know.'

'Oh, really?'

'Not physical ones,' Mrs Tennant explained. 'Deeper than that, if you know what I mean.'

Amy didn't but decided against showing too much interest. She glanced meaningfully at her watch and sent the older woman a tight smile. 'I'm sorry I wasn't able to help you today. Perhaps you'd like to book another appointment and I can conduct a more thorough investigation into your current ailments.'

'I'll think about it,' Mrs Tennant said, and, snatching up her oversized handbag, bustled out.

The door had only just closed on her exit when Allan opened it after a brief knock.

'I'm sorry to bother you, Amy...'

Amy frowned at his greyish pallor and quickly got to her feet. 'What's wrong, Allan? Are you feeling unwell?'

He gave her a sheepish look and sank to the chair in front of her desk. 'I'm sorry to do this to you, Amy, but I think I'm going to have to take a few days off. I've been pushing myself too hard for too long. Will you be able to manage for a week or so on your own? I can try and organise a locum for back-up, but you probably know how long it takes to get someone to fill these remote positions. It could take a month or more.'

'Don't worry about it, Allan,' she said. 'I can manage. But how about I check you over? How long have you been feeling unwell?'

'It's nothing serious, probably stress-related if anything. I thought I might go and stay with my daughter for a few days, maybe even head down to the Margaret River region with her for a break. Heaven knows, we both could do with it.'

'That sounds like an excellent idea,' Amy said. 'And, please, don't worry about things here. I'm sure I'll cope.'

'I'm sure you will. You did an excellent job on Bobby Williams,' Allan said. 'I couldn't have done better.'

'Thank you, but I didn't do it alone,' she said. 'Sergeant Ford was there with me.'

'He's a good cop,' Allan said as he got up to leave. 'Sharp as a tack. Nothing gets past him.'

Amy couldn't quite remove the dryness from her tone. 'So I've heard.'

'You know you really should think about moving out there with him,' he said. 'The hotel's not the place for a decent young woman like you.'

'What is it about everyone in this town insisting I live with Sergeant Ford?' she asked with an edge of frustration. 'Is this some sort of dastardly conspiracy to find him a wife?'

'You could do a lot worse than Angus,' Allan said. 'And think of how wonderful it would be if you decided to stay for longer than three months. I could finally think about retiring.'

'Sorry to disappoint you, but I don't see that happening,' she said. 'I'm not sure I can handle the intrusion into my personal life, for one thing.'

'Ah, you're referring to dear old Mona, I dare say,' he said. 'Don't take too much notice of her. She likes to have a gossip now and again. She probably only came in to see you to give you the once-over.'

Amy decided to come clean. 'Allan, I have a confession to make. I should have told you when I answered the advertisement, but I didn't want anyone to know…'

'You're Lindsay Redgrove's cousin, aren't you?' Allan said before she could continue.

'You already knew?'

He nodded. 'I spoke at length to her parents while they were here. They mentioned they had a niece who was a doctor. I have a good memory for names so when I saw yours on the application I put two and two together.'

'I'm sorry… I should have told you earlier.'

'I understand your reluctance in revealing your connection to Lindsay, that's why I didn't say anything to you and I haven't told anyone else. She was a difficult person at times.'

'Was she your patient?'

'No, Jacqui looked after her mostly.'

'Do you think it will be a problem, people finding out I'm her cousin?' Amy asked. 'I was caught off guard with Mrs Tennant and let it slip out.'

'I'd like to say that no one will hold it against you but this is a small town and it has its share of bigots,' he said. 'But from what I've seen so far, you're a highly competent and caring doctor. That's really all that matters, isn't it?'

'Thank you,' she said with a grateful smile.

He reached for the door. 'But I would seriously think again about moving in with Angus,' he said. 'You could go a long way to find a man as nice as him.'

'I *have* come a long way,' Amy said a little defensively. 'But it wasn't to find a man, even one as saintly as Sergeant Ford is reputed to be.'

'No harm in keeping your options open,' he said, and with another fatherly smile closed the door as he left.

CHAPTER NINE

AMY buried her head under the pillow for the tenth time that night as the snores from room number four reverberated through the thin walls.

She had met Maurie Morrison over dinner in the dining room, having only just scraped in on time after being held up at the clinic with a last-minute patient with an allergic reaction to a beesting. Betty, the cook, had given her a disapproving frown and placed an overloaded plate in front of her, the greasy food swimming in a congealing pool of gravy doing nothing to encourage her already diminishing appetite.

Maurie had talked non-stop about anything and everything until Amy's eyes had begun to glaze over. She had politely excused herself and gone to her room to escape into a book, but on her last visit to the bathroom before bed, she'd had to stand outside for endless minutes, practically cross-legged, until Maurie had finally come out with a sheepish grin, before shuffling back to his room, his slippers flapping on his feet.

Amy had finally got to bed, closed her eyes and drifted off to sleep, only to be woken a couple of hours later by a racket that would have got a seismologist leaping to his feet in alarm, she was sure.

She glanced at the clock after another sleepless hour and groaned. How was she supposed to be single-handedly responsible for the town's health with no sleep? She hadn't even had a chance to recover from the stress and drama of the night before.

She let another half-hour pass before she decided that rather than toss and turn any longer she would get up and do something physical. The sky was starting to lighten so she put on her trainers and a pair of shorts and top and, scooping up her car keys, tiptoed downstairs.

Without consciously intending to head that way, she suddenly found herself approaching the turn-off to Caveside Cove. She turned into the road and, leaving her car in the shade of a tree, took the rough pathway the rest of the way down to the beach.

The ocean was rolling in with a two-metre swell, the salt spray filling the fresh morning air with fine beads of moisture. The sun on the cliffs had turned them almost pink and the sand beneath her feet was littered with thousands of shells.

She cast her eyes back to the sea and watched in fascination as a dorsal fin broke the surface of the water just beyond the breakers. Within moments another one appeared and then the glistening arc of a dolphin's back surfaced. The rest of the pod was close behind, their bodies undulating with the smooth grace of nature at its perfect best.

After a while they swam out of sight and Amy's eyes moved to where her cousin's shack was situated in the dunes halfway along the beach, and before she knew it her legs were carrying her towards it.

Even in the flattering light of the golden glow of early morning the shack didn't look like a place anyone in their right mind would want to live in indefinitely.

But, then, Lindsay hadn't been in her right mind, Amy reminded herself somewhat painfully. She cast her memory back to the days when she had looked up to her older cousin before Lindsay's mental health had taken such a sudden unexpected turn. Being five years older, Lindsay had often babysat Amy when her mother had had some engagement to go to. Amy had loved the funny little pictures her cousin had drawn to entertain her and she had nothing but pleasant memories of their times together during that time.

However, it had all changed seemingly overnight when Lindsay had been in her final year of high school. She had fallen in with a rough crowd and begun to experiment with drugs, cannabis mostly. Within weeks she had started to buckle under the pressure of looming exams, spending sleepless nights in agitation and eventually missing day after day of school. She'd run away from home on more than one occasion, and her first suicide attempt had thrown Amy's aunt and uncle into an emotional tailspin they had never quite recovered from.

Amy could still recall the shock of seeing her cousin lying so ghostly white in that hospital bed, her thin wrists bandaged where she had slashed them.

Over the next few years Lindsay had been

under almost constant psychiatric monitoring, a host of drugs prescribed in an attempt to bring her out of her psychosis, but in the end nothing had really seemed to work as effectively as the move to Marraburra. It had been as if the shift away from her troubled past to the quiet coastal town on the other side of the country had been just what she'd needed to find inner peace.

Amy pushed her sadness over her cousin's tragic life aside as she tried the door of the shack, even though she knew Angus had locked it the day before.

'You really shouldn't come out here alone,' a voice said from behind her.

She felt her heart leap upwards as she swung around to see Angus standing there. 'You scared the living daylights out of me!' Her voice came out high-pitched and wobbly. 'Couldn't you have called out or something?'

'I mean it, Dr Tanner. This is an isolated, un-patrolled beach, as I told you previously. You'd be better to stick to the one closer to town if you want an early morning run or swim.'

Amy stuck up her chin. 'I can look after myself.'

His hand came up and briefly touched his

eyebrow where a shadow of a bruise was showing beneath his tan. 'Yes, I am in no doubt of that, but I still recommend you keep to the more populated areas.'

She inspected his lightweight running gear before returning her eyes to his. 'You don't seem to suffer the same reservations when choosing where to exercise,' she pointed out.

'Fergus is with me,' he said.

Amy knew he was probably right about being out there all alone. She had seen enough attacks on young women to know there was danger in being too blasé about personal safety, even in supposedly quiet country towns. But something about his demeanour made her wonder if he had his own private reasons for keeping her away from Caveside Cove, and especially away from her cousin's shack.

His dark brown gaze held hers for a pulsing moment. 'I'll walk with you back to your car,' he said.

She stood her ground. 'I'm not planning on leaving just yet.'

A brief flash of irritation passed over his features. 'Fine,' he said. 'I'll wait for you.'

'What's going on, Sergeant Ford?' she asked, her eyes narrowed at him in suspicion. 'Why don't you want me to hang around here?'

Angus could have kicked himself for being so transparent. The last thing he wanted to do was make any alarms bells ring in her head. 'You can come here any time you like,' he said evenly. 'But for your own safety it would be best if you didn't come alone.'

'My cousin lived out here all alone for a couple of years without a problem,' she said.

'Your cousin eventually committed suicide.'

Her brows rose slightly. 'Are you suggesting the loneliness got to her?'

'It would get to anyone after a while.'

She angled her head at him. 'And yet you live all by yourself on top of that cliff around at the Point, don't you, Sergeant? Tell me something, does it get to you? Do you feel yourself going stir crazy with boredom and loneliness?'

He was going crazy, lying awake at night thinking of how her soft mouth had felt beneath his, Angus thought wryly. Not to mention the sight of her gorgeous naked body which he hadn't been able to erase from his mind. 'No, it doesn't,' he said. 'And I'm not usually alone.'

'Oh, yes, you've got Fergus,' she said as the dog came up to her and snuffled her hand.

'Yes.'

Amy returned her gaze to his watchful one. 'I'd better get going. Allan's having a few days off and leaving me in charge.'

Angus frowned. 'Is he unwell?'

'I'm not exactly sure. He didn't go into details. He just said he felt a little stressed and wanted to take a break with his daughter.'

'Will you be able to manage on your own?' he asked.

'It's a small country town, Sergeant Ford,' she said, sending him a haughty look. 'I'm sure I'll manage to keep everyone alive until he gets back, in spite of what some of the locals think.'

'I heard the town's matriarch, Mona Tennant, came to see you,' he said with a ghost of a smile.

She rolled her eyes. 'Mona is right. She moaned the whole time she was there.'

'She's used to getting her way,' Angus said, and then after a little pause added, 'I think I should warn you not to tell her about your connection with Lindsay. Mona is likely to spread it around pretty widely.'

Amy gave a frown of annoyance. 'Too late,' she said. 'I wouldn't have said anything but she half guessed it anyway. She said we were seen out here on Monday and she knew we'd spent the night together.'

'And that bothered you?'

Her cheeks took on a rosy hue. 'Why should it bother me?'

He gave a tiny shrug, his eyes still locked on hers. 'You tell me.'

Amy fidgeted under his scrutiny. 'I don't like the thought of people gossiping about me.'

'Small towns like this are known for their gossip loops,' he said. 'You either get used to it or circumvent it.'

'Is that why you don't have a woman in your life?'

His eyes hardened a fraction. 'I told you my reasons.'

'Yes, you did, but I still find it hard to believe a full-blooded man like you would be content to go for months at a stretch without female company,' she said. 'The way you kissed me the other night seemed to suggest you're currently feeling the effects of the drought.'

There was a moment of tense silence broken only by the deep pulse of the ocean in the background.

'Are you offering to alleviate the boredom for me, Dr Tanner?'

Amy felt her stomach clench against the sudden kick of desire his smoothly drawled words triggered. His dark gaze smouldered as he stepped closer, his hands coming down on the tops of her shoulders as he brought her up against him in preparation for his descending mouth.

His kiss was just earth-shattering as the last time, the movement of his lips and tongue driving every rational thought out of her brain. Sexual energy fired like a surging current from his body to hers, leaving her boneless in his crushing hold.

She kissed him back with passion-charged heat, her tongue dancing around the determined thrust of his, her breasts jammed up against him, her pelvis burning where he pressed against her.

He shifted position which afforded her a chance to suck greedily on his bottom lip, the action drawing a deep guttural groan from his throat. She pushed her tongue back into his mouth as one of his hands found her breast, the warmth of his palm exploring her boldly and possessively through the thin cotton of her T-shirt.

His unshaven jaw scored her soft skin when he deepened the kiss even further, but she was beyond caring. She had never felt such over-whelming desire. Her love-making with Simon seemed so pathetically tame in comparison. She had never clawed at Simon so wantonly, never felt the scrape of teeth against her own as each kiss became more urgent, never felt her body burn and turn to liquid with such intense longing.

She sucked in a sharp almost painful breath as Angus lifted her T-shirt and moved his mouth from hers to suckle on her breast, the exquisite sensation of his lips and tongue on her naked flesh sending arrows of need to every secret part of her.

He went to her other breast and subjected it to the same passionate onslaught until she was prac-tically swaying in his arms. Her hands looked for an anchor and looped around his neck, pulling his head back down for his mouth to meet hers.

In the end it was Fergus who brought the kiss

to an end. His sharp bark from further down the beach brought Angus's head up, his eyes narrowing against the early slant of the sun as he stepped away from her.

'Excuse me,' he said, his expression becoming all cop-like and closed again.

Amy stood on unsteady legs as she watched him walk to where Fergus was standing at the base of the crumbling cliff at the far end of the beach, her heart coming to a chugging stop when she what the dog had spotted in amongst the fallen debris.

A pair of legs, the feet clad in trainers, was protruding from behind the screen of the rocks.

Angus straightened from the body and called out to her as he reached for his mobile. 'Come quickly. He's alive. I'll call the ambulance.'

Amy ran down the beach to join him, and he moved out of her way as she kneeled next to the supine body of a man in his late thirties. He was breathing, but only just, his airway almost obstructed by his tongue, his colour cyanotic and his eyes closed.

'Help me turn him onto his side,' Amy instructed, the priorities of trauma resuscitation assembling in her mind, even though her heart sank at how limited she was with no equipment at hand.

Angus assisted her in rolling the body into the coma position, Amy supporting the head and neck and providing jaw-thrust whilst Angus did most of the physical work. The manoeuvre instantly improved the airway as the stertorous breath sounds became quiet, the body breathing now in a regular rhythm as long as Amy supported the jaw.

'He's got a boggy haematoma over the occiput,' she said, not realising she was speaking aloud until she caught sight of Angus's raised brow. 'The back of his head,' she clarified.

'Right, I had noticed that,' he said.

'Can you see any other injuries? I can't let go of the airway.'

Angus began to undo the short dark-coloured cotton shirt on the body. 'No signs of any obvious chest trauma,' he said, and proceeded to the abdomen and back and then lower and upper limbs. 'There are abrasions all over his arms and legs and his back, and his ankle looks as if it's broken.'

'Do you think he's fallen from the cliff?' Amy asked as she glanced at the man's contorted ankle.

'Looks like it,' he said, looking at the man's face, a small frown bringing his brows together.

'Do you know who it is?' she asked.

He shook his head. 'Never seen him before.'

'Maybe he's a tourist…you know, out for a hike and lost his footing.'

'Maybe,' Angus answered absently as he glanced back up at the cliff face.

Amy followed the line of his gaze. 'It's a long way to fall.'

'Yeah,' he said, looking down the beach for any sign of the ambulance arriving.

A stray thought wandered into Amy's head. 'What if he was pushed?'

His eyes came back to hers. 'You've been watching too many cop shows, Dr Tanner.'

She found his tone a little condescending and pursed her mouth at him. 'So you don't think there's anything suspicious about this?' she asked.

'A full and proper investigation will be carried out in due course. Let's hope he lives long enough to tell us what he was doing up there in the first place. For all we know, he might have jumped.'

Amy's eyes clashed momentarily with his. 'Yet

another suicide, Sergeant Ford? Isn't that rather a coincidence?'

'What are you suggesting, Dr Tanner?'

She raised her chin a fraction. 'You were the one to report my cousin's death as suicide, weren't you?'

His gaze hardened as it collided with hers. 'And your point is?'

'What if you got it wrong?' she asked. 'What if she didn't commit suicide at all? What if someone murdered her and made it look like a suicide?'

'You're letting your emotions rule your head,' he said. 'It's understandable because she was your cousin, but let me assure you the proper channels of investigation were followed at all times, as they will be in this case as well.'

'I don't believe Lindsay took her own life and I'm not going to rest until I find out who killed her.'

'Then you'll be wasting your time because the results of my investigation and the decision of the coroner were one and the same. It was suicide and the sooner you accept it the better.'

'There has hardly been a police investigation that I can tell,' she threw back. 'It seems to me a verdict of suicide was reached before a proper investigation was carried out.'

'You are welcome to see the records on the investigation.'

Amy wondered if he was calling her bluff. She hunted his face but it was hard to tell what he was thinking behind the screen of his dark, unreadable eyes.

The rest of their conversation was interrupted by the arrival of the volunteer ambulance officers who drove as close as they could to the cliff base before removing the spinal board from the back of the four wheel drive vehicle.

'The Flying Doctor's been called up to Monkey Mia for a mild case of hypothermia—some guy stayed down too long on a dive,' Joan said. 'The doctor accompanying the patient said they'll stop in to pick up this guy on the way back. It'll be quicker than the paramedics anyway.'

As they were transferring the man into the ambulance a police vehicle arrived and a man of similar age to Angus came over to speak to them.

'Anyone we know?' James Ridley asked Angus after brief introductions were made.

'No,' Angus said. 'But it looks like he might

have been there overnight. He was lucky the tide didn't take him out to sea.'

'He was fortunate you and Dr Tanner found him when you did,' James said with a speculative glance in Amy's direction. 'So what brought you way out here so early in the morning?'

Amy felt her colour rise. 'I was out…er… walking and ran into Sergeant Ford.'

James's gaze swung back to his colleague, his hazel eyes twinkling. 'I'd better get back to town. I'll let you see Dr Tanner back to her car.' He turned back to address Amy. 'Nice to meet you, Dr Tanner. My wife is really keen to meet you. I'll have a word with her and see if we can organise something soon.'

'That would be very nice,' she said, smiling weakly.

Angus walked her back to her car once James had left. 'I was expecting you to tell Senior Constable Ridley what we were doing prior to finding the body,' he said with a glint of devilment in his eyes. 'Why didn't you?'

She stopped to look up at him in shock. 'You surely don't think I would reveal something like that!'

He gave her a smouldering look as he opened her car door for her. 'So you prefer to keep what goes on between us private, do you?'

'There is *nothing* going on between us,' Amy said sternly. 'It was just a kiss and not a part—'

His fingertip came over her lips to silence her, the ironic glint in his eyes sending her senses into a tailspin. 'Don't say it, Dr Tanner, otherwise I might be tempted to make you eat those words of yours the next time.'

He lifted his finger from her mouth and, stepping back from her, whistled to Fergus.

'There's *not* going to be a next time,' she bit out determinedly, but he had already begun walking back the way he'd come.

CHAPTER TEN

NEWS of the injured man's body on the beach was all over town by the time Amy got to the clinic.

'What a ghastly shock for you!' Helen said. 'Just as well Sergeant Ford was with you at the time.'

'Er…yes…'

Helen gave her a probing look. 'So what *were* you doing out there with him at that time of the morning?' she asked.

Amy wished she had some way of turning off her tendency to blush at the mere mention of Angus's name. 'I went for a walk and…er…ran into him there.'

'I expect you went out there to visit your cousin's shack.' There was a hint of pique in the receptionist's tone.

'I'm sorry I didn't tell you the first day,' Amy said. 'I didn't want to make it public knowledge.'

'Yes, well, Mona is like a gossip hotline so your secret is well and truly out now.'

Amy caught her lip for a moment. 'I hope it's not going to be a negative thing, you know, people knowing Lindsay and I were related. Allan Peddington said it shouldn't make a difference but I'm not so sure.'

'I shouldn't think it will be a problem,' Helen reassured her. 'Lindsay was a bit of an oddball admittedly, but that doesn't mean people will expect you to be the same.'

Amy decided to take the bull by the horns. 'You mentioned that first day that no one expected her to take her life. Do you think there's any possibility that she didn't commit suicide?'

Helen's face visibly paled. 'You mean someone could have...murdered her?'

Amy nodded.

'But the police and the coroner—'

'They could have got it wrong,' Amy said. 'You hinted at it yourself the other day.'

'No,' Helen insisted. 'I just said Lindsay's parents seemed resigned to the fact she was going to do it some day.'

'But that's exactly my point,' Amy argued. 'How easy would it be to pass off murder as a suicide in someone who had been suicidal in the past?'

Helen's expression became guarded. 'I don't think you should spread that opinion around too freely. The police work hard enough out here as it is, without someone from outside questioning every detail of a case that was open and shut from the start.' She straightened her spine and added stiffly, 'The first patients are here. I think we should get on with treating the living instead of speculating about the dead.'

Amy let out a slow breath as she picked up the first patient's file.

It was going to be a long and tiring day.

Just as she was preparing to leave for the afternoon she heard a commotion in Reception, raised voices and furniture being knocked over.

Her door burst open and Helen's worried face appeared. 'Quick, Amy,' she said. 'We've got an emergency. I've called the police and they're on their way.'

Amy rushed out to find a harried father trying to control his teenage son, who was kicking and shouting and swearing volubly, his eyes wild and glazed.

'Help him!' the father cried in panic as he half carried, half dragged the lad into the examination room. 'I think he's taken something. He's gone crazy.'

Amy tried to keep her own panic under control as she tried to avoid the boy's flailing arms and legs.

'Get away! Don't touch me!' the boy screamed at the top of his voice, and fought viciously against his father's iron hold.

Amy felt her stomach clench as the boy's hand came up and punched his father full in the face, the crunch of fist on the man's nose making her own eyes water as the blood began to spurt. The blow loosened the man's hold on his son and the boy rushed for the door but came up against Angus and James, who together managed to restrain him.

'Come on, Hamish,' Angus said in a calm voice. 'It's all right, mate.'

'Let me go!' the boy wailed, his eyes frantic with fear. 'They're eating me alive! Oh, God! There are hundreds of them!'

'Can you hold him down on the treatment table?' Amy directed. 'He's obviously hallucinating.' She turned to the father who was holding his nose with a wad of tissues Helen had handed him. 'Do you have any idea of what your son has taken?'

The father was openly weeping now, and shook his head helplessly. James let out a grunt of pain as Hamish's knee caught him in the groin and he momentarily dropped his hold.

'It looks like crystal meth,' Angus said, putting his whole weight across the boy to hold him down while his colleague got his breath back.

'That's what I was thinking, too,' Amy said. 'Can you hold him while I get an IV in?'

He nodded and then winced as Hamish tried to bite his arm. 'Cool it, Hamish. Dr Tanner is here to help you.'

Amy struggled to insert an IV with the boy bucking and rolling. Somehow she got it in and administered 5 mg midazolam but there was virtually no affect. Hamish kept swearing and in spite of the two police officers doing their level best to restrain him, he appeared to have almost superhuman strength. He almost got out from under them and in his attempt to secure his hold

Angus shifted position, allowing the boy's arms to suddenly flail upwards, jerking Angus's elbow back against Amy's cheek.

'Sorry,' he gritted out as he tightened his hold, sending a quick concerned glance over his shoulder, his face pinched and strained. 'Did I hurt you?'

'I'm all right but I need to give him more,' she said, and titrated another 5 mg, which began to take effect almost immediately. Hamish's jerking limbs began to relax and within minutes he was sleeping.

'Is he going to be all right?' the father asked, still holding his bleeding nose.

Amy led him to a vacant chair and helped him to sit down. 'Your son will need to be kept under observation,' she said. 'We don't have the facilities here so I'd like to send him to Geraldton. Crystal meth, or "ice" is a highly toxic drug with a whole host of frightening side effects, some of which you just witnessed—psychosis, extreme violence and hallucinations.'

'I don't know where he got it,' the father said, glancing nervously towards the police officers. 'I swear to God I don't.'

'I'd better see to that nose of yours,' Amy said,

and lifted off the blood-soaked pad. The bleeding had stopped but when Amy moved the nasal bones from side to side, there was obvious crepitus, indicating a fracture. 'I'll need to put a plaster bridge across your nose to stabilise it,' she said. 'Helen, can you go get the plaster trolley?'

'I've called the Flying Doctor,' Helen said as she came back in with the trolley. 'The road ambulance will be here to transfer him to the airfield in ten minutes.'

'Thanks, Helen,' Amy said, inwardly quailing at the thought of another stomach-churning journey in that tiny aircraft. She met Angus's dark brown gaze and felt her cheeks flare with colour. She'd been lucky that morning with a doctor already on board offering to escort the cliff-fall man to Geraldton, but now it looked as if she was going to have to face her winged demons again.

'It might be best if someone else goes with Hamish,' Angus said. 'With Allan Peddington away, it leaves the town vulnerable in case of an emergency.'

Amy could have kissed him right there in front of everyone.

'He'll be all right, won't he?' the father asked. 'I mean, nothing could go wrong now, could it?'

'The midazolam will probably keep him sedated until he gets to Geraldton,' Amy said, 'But I'll leave the canula in and send another ampoule of midazolam with him in case he needs further sedation *en route*. The physicians in Geraldton will keep him monitored overnight— he should come through relatively unscathed. But I would recommend some sessions with a drug counsellor. There have been cases where just a single drug use like this has triggered schizophrenia.'

'He's never done this before,' the father said. 'Will he be charged?'

'We'll sort that out later, Rob,' Angus said. 'He's only fifteen so any action taken will be through diversionary conferencing and counselling. But for now you'd better prepare to go with Hamish. Do you want me to call Janelle for you?'

'She's going to kill me for this,' Rob said. 'Trust it to happen when he's with me on a custody visit.'

Angus put his hand on Rob's shoulder. 'Try not to blame yourself, mate. You did the right thing in getting him here quickly. It could have been much worse.'

Amy applied a plaster of Paris strip across Rob Norton's nose while they waited for the ambulance, and once it was on its way, with both father and son on board, James came over to speak to her.

'I spoke to Jacqui, Dr Tanner. She suggested you come around for a barbecue tonight. You, too, Angus,' he said turning back to his colleague. 'That way you can drive so Amy doesn't get lost.'

'I'm sure I can find my own way there if Sergeant Ford is busy this evening,' Amy put in quickly.

'It's fine,' Angus said, sending her one of his inscrutable looks. 'I've got nothing planned. What time do you want us out there?'

'How about seven?' James said. 'Then at least you'll get to see Daisy before she goes to sleep for the night.'

'Seven's fine,' Angus answered for her.

'See you both, then,' James said, lifting his hand in a wave.

Amy turned to leave but Angus stalled her with a hand on her arm. 'It looks to me like you need some ice on that cheek,' he said.

She gave a little shudder. '*Please,* don't mention that word.'

His finger gently brushed the purpling bruise on her cheekbone just below her eye. 'Does it hurt?' he asked.

Not when you do that, Amy thought. 'Not much,' she said. 'It wasn't your fault. I should have got out of the way.'

'I'm sorry you got caught in the crossfire. He was hard to control. They always are.'

'You've had a bit of experience with this, haven't you?'

A shutter came down over his eyes. 'It's part of the job. Yours, too, I imagine. We've both seen things we'd prefer not to have seen.'

'Yes…' she said, stifling a little yawn.

'Am I keeping you awake, Dr Tanner?' he asked.

'I haven't slept more than two hours in a stretch since I arrived,' she confessed. 'That's why I was out so early this morning. I had no idea the old man in the next room could snore at seven on the Richter scale.'

'Yeah, well, I had someone keeping me awake, too,' he said, his eyes going to the soft curve of her mouth.

'Oh?' she said, moistening her lips with the tip of her tongue. 'Who was it?'

'Are you searching for a compliment, Dr Tanner?' he asked with a glint in his dark eyes.

'Are you going to give me one?' she asked.

He didn't answer immediately, but Amy felt his darker-than-night gaze move over her lazily, as if he was slowly removing every article of clothing from her to look at her, making every hair of her skin lift in feverish anticipation.

'Don't you think it's time we dropped the formalities?' he said and gave her his hand. 'Hi, I'm Angus.'

She bit back a giggle as she shook his hand. 'Hi, Angus, I'm Amy.'

'Nice to meet you, Amy.'

'Me, too,' she said, and blushed then rambled on gauchely, 'I mean, you, too. It's nice to meet *you*, not me…well, you know what I mean.'

He smiled a slow smile that made his eyes darken even further. 'I know exactly what you mean.' He put his police hat back on and tipped it at her. 'See you tonight. I'll pick you up at six-forty.'

Amy let out a prickly breath as she watched him stride towards his car. *So what if he's a cop?* she began mentally rehearsing her explanation to her mother. He's the first and only man I've been attracted to since Simon. So what if it's only going to last three months? I'm a modern single girl. It doesn't mean I have to fall in love with him.

I'm not going to be *that* stupid.

She pulled her shoulders back with determination.

No way.

CHAPTER ELEVEN

'Off out this evening?' Bill asked as Amy came downstairs at six-thirty on the dot.

'Yes, to James and Jacqui Ridley's house.'

'Sounds like a good idea after that drama out at the Cove this morning,' he said. 'Do you need directions? It's a bit hard to find. I can draw you a map if you like.'

Amy felt a slow burn crawl over her cheeks. 'Um…it's all right,' she said. 'I'm getting a lift with someone.'

Bill's eyes began to twinkle. 'That would be Sergeant Ford, right?'

'Yes, but there's nothing—'

'It's about time that lad took his mind off work for a change,' Bill cut her off as he gave the counter a quick wipe. 'I don't think he's been on a date since he called off his engagement when he came out here a couple of years ago.'

'He was engaged?' The question popped out before Amy could stop it.

'Yeah, to a woman back in Perth.'

'So what happened?'

Bill opened his mouth to speak when the door of the pub opened behind Amy. He looked past her and smiled. 'G'day, Sarge. I hear you're taking Dr Tanner out on a date.'

Amy felt like sinking under the bar.

'Is that what she told you?' Angus asked.

She swung around, her colour still high. 'No, of course I didn't tell him that.'

His eyes ran over her pink cotton skirt and white halter top, pausing for a moment on the thrust of her breasts. 'Are you ready?' he asked.

'Yes,' she said, and, snatching up her purse and the chocolates and wine she'd bought earlier, walked stiffly out to the car.

Angus held the passenger door open for her. 'Don't take any notice of Bill,' he said. 'He likes to think of himself as a bit of a matchmaker.'

'He told me you used to be engaged,' she said once they were on their way. 'Funny that you didn't mention that the other night when I told you about my ex-fiancé.'

'I didn't think it was relevant.'

She turned to look at him. 'Why did you break it off?'

His eyes were fixed on the road ahead. 'I changed my mind.'

'Simple as that?'

'Yeah.'

'How did she take it?' she asked.

He lifted one shoulder in a shrug. 'Pretty well as it turned out. She found someone else within a matter of weeks.'

'Were you upset?'

'Why should I be?'

She frowned at him. 'I don't know. Even though you were the one to break it off, I imagine it would have still hurt a bit that she replaced you so quickly.'

'As far as I was concerned, she was a free agent. It was none of my business any more what she did or who she did it with.'

'You're very good at switching off your emotions when you want to, aren't you?' she asked. 'Did you love her?'

'Define what you mean by the word "love".'

Amy gave a choked sound of cynicism. 'Now,

that's just absolutely typical. What is it about men that they refuse to acknowledge how deeply a woman affects them?'

'Were you in love with your ex?' he said.

'What sort of question is that? Of course I was in love with him.'

'Are you still in love with him?'

She hesitated over her answer. 'Um….no.'

'It can't have been the real thing if it died just because one person called a halt to the relationship,' he said. 'Don't you agree?'

Amy wasn't sure how to answer. She had thought she had been in love with Simon, truly in love, but she could barely recall what he even looked like now. And as for his kisses and caresses…well, they had been eradicated from her memory by the heat and fire of Angus's.

'What about time being a great healer and all that?' she asked.

'I'm not a great believer in that particular adage. I think people only say it because they can't think of anything else to say.'

'But don't you think it's a waste of time pining over a lost love when you could be out finding someone much more suitable?' she asked.

'Is that what you are doing?' he asked. 'Looking for someone else?'

'Not consciously,' she said. 'Although I guess you could say I'm keeping my options open.'

He sent her a quick sideways glance, his dark brown eyes gleaming. 'So you haven't quite ruled out a short-term fling with me.'

She angled her head at him. 'I thought you said you weren't in the market for a relationship.'

'I said I wasn't in the market for anything long term, but that's not to say I wouldn't be interested in working on lifting your assessment of my kisses to something other than "not particularly good".'

'Are you flirting with me, Sergeant Ford?' she asked.

His mouth stretched into a half-smile as he took the next turn that led to a house overlooking another beach further along the coast. 'Let's just say I'm keeping my options open.'

James came out to meet them, carrying his tiny daughter in his arms. 'Bang on time,' he said, handing the baby to Angus who had already reached out for her.

Amy felt a funny sensation flow through her

as she watched Angus cradle the tiny pink bundle close to his broad chest, his finger tipping up the little dimpled chin as he greeted her. 'How are you doing, Daisy? Have you got a smile for your godfather?'

'If she does, it's probably just wind,' said a pragmatic female voice from behind Amy.

Amy turned and saw a woman a couple of years older than herself come towards her with a smile. 'Hi, you must be Amy. I'm Jacqui. Welcome to Marraburra.'

'Hi, Jacqui,' she said. 'This is very good of you, organising a barbecue at such short notice.'

'Not at all.' Jacqui smiled. 'I've been dying to meet you but I'm afraid I haven't made it into town to do so yet. I don't know where the day goes. I swore I would never be one of those new mums who spend the whole day in their dressing-gowns, but Daisy clearly hasn't read the same baby-care manuals as I have.'

Amy laughed at the woman's self-effacing humour. 'I've heard it said that the only people who say they slept like a baby haven't had one.'

Jacqui rolled her eyes expressively. 'Tell me about it. And here I was thinking one in two on call was bad. The other night Daisy kept me up longer than any patient I've ever had.'

'She's beautiful,' Amy said, looking at the gurgling infant, who was tugging with a dimpled hand at the front of Angus's shirt.

'Well, we think so, don't we, darling?' Jacqui said as she snuggled under her husband's outstretched arm.

James's smile for his wife, Amy decided, would be enough to restore anyone's dented belief in true love. It was clear they adored each other and the bond of their child only added to it.

'I heard you both had a pretty gruelling start to the day.' Jacqui addressed both Amy and Angus. 'Has the man's identity been established yet?'

Angus shook his head as he repositioned the baby in his arms. 'Not as yet. No one's reported him missing and he wasn't carrying any ID.'

'Do you think it could be one of the drug mules?' Jacqui asked.

'Drug mules?' Amy asked with a frown.

James exchanged a glance with Angus and after a tiny pause Jacqui took Amy by the arm and led her to the kitchen. 'Come and have a chat with me in the kitchen while the boys talk shop.'

Amy followed but not before sending Angus a quizzical look which, she noted, he pointedly ignored. She followed Jacqui into the large kitchen and at her hostess's direction perched on one of the bar stools surrounding the island bench.

'I guess you haven't heard,' Jacqui said as she took the plastic film off a bowl of salad.

'Heard what?'

'This part of the coast is well known for South-East Asian drug drop-offs,' Jacqui said. 'Heroin mostly. The drugs are off-loaded out at sea and collected by fishing boats and then taken to Perth for redistribution. It's becoming a huge problem over here. So much of the coast is unguarded. Angus and James and the other constables do what they can, but it's not enough to stop such a big operation.'

'So they think the man we found this morning is somehow connected?' Amy asked.

'Could be, but until they find out who he is, who knows? Besides, he might not recover. James was saying he had a pretty nasty head injury.'

'Yes, he hasn't regained consciousness, as far as I know.'

'James was telling me young Hamish Norton

was in earlier out of his head on crystal meth. That would have been pretty scary. We've never had anything like that to deal with before.'

'It was awful,' Amy said unable to suppress a small shudder. 'I've seen it before in London. Perfectly normal kids turn into violent animals. But this was the first time I'd had to deal with it medically on my own, although James and Angus were there, as you know.'

Jacqui's green eyes went to the bruise on Amy's cheek. 'Is that how you got that?' she asked.

'Yes. Angus was trying to hold him down but Hamish was all legs and arms.'

'Not a great first week for you,' Jacqui said, 'especially with Allan taking time off. It makes me feel guilty for taking maternity leave.'

'I'm fine, really,' Amy assured her. 'And you shouldn't be feeling guilty for wanting to spend time with your new baby. It's a very special time in your life.'

'Yes, and I'm almost dreading returning to full-time work,' Jacqui said, and then with an impish look added, 'I don't suppose we could tempt you into staying longer than three months?'

Amy felt a wave of guilty colour wash over her.

'I'm sure you'll find out sooner or later that the only reason I came here was to see the place my cousin Lindsay Redgrove lived and died.'

Jacqui's eyes widened. 'So it is true. I heard a rumour that you were Lindsay's cousin but I decided to wait to hear it from you first.' Her expression clouded as she added, 'She was my patient, you know. It was such a shock when she took her life. I'd only seen her the week before and she seemed on top of things.'

'Did she have any relapses into psychosis during the time she lived here?' Amy asked.

'Now and again she'd go off the rails a bit,' Jacqui answered. 'She had her ups and downs but she was really good about taking her medication, almost obsessive about it really, as if she was frightened of going back to the dark days of her adolescence. I believe it was a very frightening time for her as well as for her parents. She told me a little about it, the regrets she had about her drug use and so on.'

'It was a frightening horrible time,' Amy said. 'She went from a normal well-adjusted girl to a paranoid stranger almost overnight.'

'They've obviously had it tough, as do any

parents struggling to cope with a child with mental illness,' Jacqui said.

'Yes, it was hard on everyone. My mother felt guilty that it was her sister's daughter and not hers who had the problem. I felt it, too. There I was off at university, doing a medical degree, while my only cousin was spending most of her young adult years in and out of psychiatric wards.'

'Survivor guilt is a very common reaction,' Jacqui said. 'But you mustn't blame yourself for making something of your life.'

'No, I guess not.'

'So, has coming here helped?' Jacqui asked. 'Has it answered any questions about her for you?'

'On the contrary, it's thrown up a whole lot more,' Amy confessed.

'What do you mean?'

Amy took a small breath and announced, 'I'm not one hundred per cent convinced Lindsay committed suicide.'

Jacqui stared at her with wide green eyes. 'But Angus and James did the preliminary report and the coroner agreed it was a straight case of suicide.'

'I know but I can't help feeling there's something not quite right about it all. She was happy here and settled for the first time in over a decade. I can't believe she would throw it all away without showing some sign first, but everyone I've spoken to says the same thing— she seemed perfectly OK even up to a couple of days before.'

'Yes, but you and I both know how quickly things can change in someone struggling with fluctuating serotonin levels,' Jacqui pointed out.

'But you said Lindsay was very good at medicating herself, which would have kept such fluctuations under control.'

'Look, Amy,' Jacqui said with a concerned expression, 'it's understandable you'd be shocked and upset about your cousin's death, but things could get awkward out here for you if you start questioning the verdict. This is a very small community. Can you imagine the impact on the locals if your suspicions became known? You're virtually accusing one of them of being a murderer.'

'I'm well aware of the delicate nature of this, but I feel I owe it to Lindsay to make sure something hasn't been overlooked somewhere.'

'I guess I'd feel the same if it was my cousin,' Jacqui finally conceded, and then, changing the subject, asked, 'So how's it going, staying at the hotel? I bet it's a bit of an eye-opener, what with Carl's bender the other day.'

'Eye-opener is right,' Amy said with a wry grimace. 'I haven't slept more than an hour at a time the whole time I've been here and I thought being a resident was bad.'

'What about boarding with Angus? He's got a spare room now that the engineer from Broome has gone back. It would be much more comfortable for you and certainly less noisy.'

'I wish I had a dollar for every time someone has suggested I move in with him,' she said a little sourly.

'So why don't you?'

The sound of the men coming into the kitchen interrupted the conversation at that point, and Amy turned when Angus asked her if she would like to hold the baby.

'I'd love to,' she said, and reached for the gurgling infant.

In transferring the squirming baby from his arms to hers, one of Angus's hands brushed against Amy's breast. Her eyes met his briefly, the electric pulse of his touch showing in the delicate colour in her cheeks.

'Sorry,' he said.

'It's all right,' she said, and, securing the bundle in her arms, looked down at the baby instead of Angus's all-seeing gaze. 'Isn't she gorgeous?'

'She certainly is,' Angus said, even though his eyes weren't on Daisy at that point.

'How about a drink?' James asked into the small silence. 'Amy? A glass of wine or something soft?'

'No alcohol for me, I'm afraid,' Amy said. 'I'm currently the only doctor in town.'

'None for me either,' Angus said. 'I gave Don and Tim the night off.'

'You work too hard,' Jacqui admonished him fondly. 'When are you going to take some time off and relax?'

'I'll get around to it some time.'

'I was telling Amy she should take your spare room for the time she's here,' Jacqui said. 'The company would do you both good.'

'I'm fine at the hotel,' Amy said quickly.

'Look at those shadows underneath her eyes,

Angus,' Jacqui said. 'What that girl needs is a decent night's sleep. Can't you think of a way to convince her to change her mind?'

'Dr Tanner is determined to tough it out with the spiders and snorers at the Dolphin View,' he said with a glinting glance in her direction. 'Aren't you, Dr Tanner?'

Amy sent him a blistering glare. 'You said you wouldn't tell anyone.'

'Tell anyone what?' Jacqui asked, as she took Daisy from Amy's arms as the infant startled to grizzle.

'I have a bit of a phobia,' Amy said, still glaring at Angus. 'Which Sergeant Ford seems to think is highly amusing.'

'Oh, Angus,' Jacqui laughed. 'You monstrous brute. Leave the poor girl alone. I don't like spiders myself. Don't pay any attention to him, Amy.'

'Food's ready,' James announced, as he came in from the barbecue area branding a pair of tongs and a tray of succulent meat and fish. 'And what's this I hear about spiders?'

'I'll tell you later,' Jacqui said with a hushing motion.

Amy got to her feet and, sending Angus another blistering look, brushed past to where James had begun to set out the meal.

CHAPTER TWELVE

AMY waited until they were on their way back to town from the Ridleys' house to vent her spleen. 'I should have known you'd spill the beans,' she said. 'No doubt it will be all over town by morning.'

'Jacqui and James wouldn't dream of telling anyone so you needn't worry on their account.'

She threw him a caustic look. 'Is there anyone else you've told?'

'No.'

She gave a cynical snort. 'I suppose the next thing you'll be doing is planting a spider somewhere just to entertain yourself with my reaction.'

'That would be a very cruel thing to do,' he said, and after a little pause added, 'I'm sorry I let it slip. It won't happen again.'

She shifted her mouth from side to side, wondering whether she should believe him.

'Has that happened to you in the past?' he asked into the silence. 'Has someone exploited you by entertaining themselves with your fear?'

Amy swung her gaze in his direction, yet again surprised by his percipience. 'Do they teach sixth sense at the police academy these days, or is that a talent you've picked up along the way?' she asked.

He sent her a half-smile. 'You provide all the clues, Amy. There's nothing intuitive about it really, just a process of adding one and one together and coming up with two.'

She looked out of the window as the shadow of the scrub passed by. 'My father hated all forms of weakness,' she said in a thread-like voice. 'He wanted a son and was quite open about his disappointment when my mother produced a daughter instead. He always acted as if she had done it deliberately, you know, to thwart his wishes, even though every one knows it is the father's Y chromosome that determines the sex of a baby.'

Angus let her continue without interruption, somehow sensing she needed to get some things off her chest.

'I was about four or five when I had a bad experience with a spider,' she said. 'I woke up to find one on my pillow. It totally freaked me out. I made the mistake of showing my fear to my father…'

Angus felt his stomach clench for what she must have suffered, but still he remained silent.

'He decided I needed to be toughened up,' she went on. 'My mother did everything she could to stop him but he was very clever at leaving his so-called desensitising sessions for whenever she wasn't around.'

'You poor little kid.' The words left his mouth before he could pull them back.

'It was a relief when my parents finally divorced,' she said. 'Of course, my father never forgave me for refusing to go on access visits.'

Angus pulled into the side of the road and turned off the engine, his eyes meeting hers in the moonlit darkness. 'No wonder you hate cops so much.'

She gave him a watery smile. 'I guess they're not all like my father.'

His hand reached for the side of her face, cupping her cheek with his palm and long fingers. 'No, they're not.'

Amy felt the slow burn of his gaze into hers,

her stomach unfolding as he leaned closer, his hint-of-mint breath whispering over her face as she closed her eyes for the touchdown of his mouth on hers.

His kiss was soft and sensual and leisurely, stirring her into a melting pool of longing as her arms reached for him, looping around his neck to hold him close. His tongue invited hers to dance with his, the sexy tango lighting spot fires all over her skin. Her thighs trembled with the pulse of need building deep inside her, and her breasts became heavy and aching for his touch.

He dragged his mouth from hers to kiss the side of her neck, his tongue tasting the lingering scent of her perfume before going lower to the shadow of cleavage her halter top revealed.

She felt the brush of his mouth against the upper curve of her breasts and instantly wanted more, her nipples tightening almost painfully in anticipation of the rasp of his tongue and sexy scrape of his teeth against them.

'I want you so badly,' he said into the throbbing silence. 'I can't seem to stop it, no matter what I do to distract myself.'

'I know…' Her breath came out on a prickly sigh. 'I want you, too.'

He pulled back to look at her in the moonlit darkness. 'Come back to my place,' he said. 'Let's enjoy this while we can.'

Out of the depths of her being a periscope of morality reared its unwelcome head and reminded Amy of the heartbreak of a no-strings relationship. Hadn't she learned enough about herself to know there was nothing about her that was without strings? She wanted strings. She wanted permanent strings.

She bit her lip and edged away, unable to hold his gaze. 'I'm sorry, Angus,' she said, staring down at her hands. 'I didn't mean to give you the wrong impression. You'll probably find this hard to believe but I'm not normally so…so… unrestrained.'

'It's OK, I understand,' he said. 'I've been acting a little out of character myself.'

'I don't blame you for being angry with me… I shouldn't have allowed things to go this far.'

'I'm not angry with you.'

She blinked up at him. 'Not even a little bit?'

He brushed the back of his knuckles over the

smooth curve of her cheek. 'Not at all,' he said. 'Unlike some men I've locked up in the past, I don't have a problem with the word "no".'

'All the same, I bet you haven't heard it too many times.'

'Now and again,' he said as he leaned back across to restart the car. 'But in every case it wasn't a big deal.'

Amy couldn't help feeling she was being relegated to the same category—no big deal. She sat back in her seat and did what she could to bolster her dented ego, reminding herself that he had never offered her anything but a short-term fling, so there was no sense in feeling affronted by his easy acceptance of her refusal to commit herself physically.

It wasn't as if she was in love with him or anything, she lectured herself severely. She was attracted to him but what woman wouldn't be? Especially seeing the way he'd held little Daisy so gently. It was enough to turn any female to mush. And his mouth was one of those mouths you couldn't stop staring at, the fullness of his bottom lip so sensual it made her insides quiver just thinking about the way it had connected with hers so intimately. And then there were those impossibly dark eyes that burned with the naked flame of desire or hardened to cold diamond chips in anger.

His hands were just as unforgettable. Strong and tanned and dusted with masculine hair that made her smooth skin tingle at the slightest touch. His body was a wall of muscle, toned and powerful, making her legs weaken at the thought of how it would feel to have him possess her…

Amy gave herself a mental slap for being so pathetic as to daydream about a man who had no interest in her other than as a temporary diversion.

'Oh, no, not again,' Angus said as the hotel came into view.

Amy looked up to see Carl stumbling from the front door of the pub, the sound of his swearing clearly audible even from inside the car.

'What are you going to do?' she asked as she got out of the car with him.

He held up the breathalyser machine he had in his hand. 'I'm going to make sure he doesn't get behind the wheel of his car.'

Amy watched as he strode over to the beat-up

car the man was trying to unlock, his attempts being hampered by his unsteady legs and lack of hand-eye coordination.

'Don't do it, Carl,' Angus said. 'I don't want to have to charge you with driving under the influence.'

The man swayed on his feet as he turned to face him. 'G'day Sarge,' he slurred. 'Can't seem to get my car unlocked. Wanna give me a hand?'

'You're not really thinking of driving tonight, are you?' Angus asked.

'Why not?' Carl gave him a belligerent look. 'It's my car.'

'How much have you had to drink?'

'Not mush.'

'How much?'

'Go on, give me a break, Sarge,' Carl growled. 'I wanna go home and you can't stop me.'

'Don't bet on it, Carl. How about you blow into the machine and then we'll come to a decision on whether or not you're fit to drive?'

Amy watched as Angus held the breathalyser for Carl, the look on Angus's face clearly indicating the man was over the legal limit.

'Sorry, mate,' Angus said. 'I can't let you drive

when you're blowing one point one. You can pick up your car tomorrow. I'll run you home.'

Carl glanced at Amy, still standing a few feet away from the car. 'So who's your new girlfriend, Sarge?' he asked, and then, squinting, added, 'Isn't that the chick that was in the pub the other day?'

'Yes, but she's not my girlfriend,' Angus answered.

'Who is she?'

'She's the new locum doctor filling in for Jacqui Ridley.'

'Nice-looking, though, isn't she?' Carl said.

Angus bundled him into the back seat. 'You're drunk, Carl,' he said dryly. 'Just about anyone would look attractive to you in this state.'

Amy sent him a fulminating glare over the top of the car 'Goodnight, Sergeant Ford,' she clipped out coldly.

A corner of his mouth tipped upwards, his dark brown eyes glinting. 'Goodnight, Dr Tanner.'

She turned on her heel and stalked into the hotel before she was tempted to say anything else.

The next week went past without Amy seeing Angus and it wasn't until Jacqui came in to see

her with Daisy for a check-up that she heard he
had gone to Perth for a few days on a police
matter.

'Didn't he tell you?' Jacqui said as she began
to dress the baby again.

'No but it's not as if we—'

'Don't bother denying it.' Jacqui cut her off
with a knowing grin. 'Everyone can see it a mile
off. You're both seriously attracted to each other.
There are bets going back and forth on how long
it will take for you to give in.'

'Oh, for God's sake!' Amy said, folding her
arms crossly. 'I don't even like the man.'

Jacqui's smile widened. 'You sound just like I
did when I first met my James. He pulled me
over and gave me a ticket for failing to indicate.
I was so angry about that it took me months to
realise how nice he really was. We got called out
to an accident late one night and I saw him with
new eyes. He was so caring and considerate of
the young child who had been injured. I invited
him around to dinner a few nights later and we
ended up in bed together.' She pressed a soft
kiss to Daisy's forehead and added, 'That's how
we got you, isn't it, my precious?'

'You mean you fell pregnant on the first date?' Amy gasped.

Jacqui's smile was sheepish. 'I may be a doctor but I'm still human. Besides, condoms have a failure rate, right?'

'Er…right…'

'You could do a lot worse, you know,' Jacqui said as she tucked the baby back into the pram. 'He needs someone like you. His ex-fiancée was totally wrong for him. She wanted him to leave the police force and get a nine-to-five job, but Angus is a cop through and through. He loves his job, in spite of the long hours and associated stress.' She straightened from the pram and added, 'Cops are like doctors when you think about it. We have to deal with the most awful stuff at times and yet carry on as if nothing's wrong.'

'I guess you're right,' Amy said. 'It's just that my father was a cop so I'm a bit prejudiced. He wasn't…I mean *isn't* a very nice person.'

'I wonder sometimes how any of them maintain normal lives,' Jacqui said. 'James is pretty level-headed, as is Angus, but they both carry a lot of baggage, Angus particularly.' She paused for a moment before continuing, 'I probably shouldn't tell you without checking with him first, but he lost his partner in a high-speed chase a couple of years ago. They were tailing a well-known drug dealer but a rogue car came out of nowhere and cut them off. Angus had to be dragged away from Daniel Fergusson's body in the end. He'd staunched the bleeding as best he could but it was too late. Dan bled out before the paramedics could get there.'

Amy felt her stomach clench. 'He said he'd named Fergus after a loyal friend... I had no idea...'

'Not only that,' Jacqui went on gravely, 'Angus was the first one on the scene of Carl's wife's accident. Julie and the girls were killed instantly when a young woman in a high-performance sports car hit them head on. The woman's father was a hotshot lawyer in Perth and got her off a dangerous driving charge. Angus was the one who had to tell Carl his family had been killed.'

Amy felt the sharp knife of guilt pierce her for assuming Angus was yet another power-hungry cop. No wonder he had taken such an instant dislike to her that first day, especially with her don't-mess-with-me-I'm-a-doctor attitude.

'I wish I'd known earlier…' She bit her lip. 'I've done nothing but insult him the whole time I've been in town. I've been far nicer to his dog than to him.'

'He really loves that dog, doesn't he?' Jacqui said with a little smile.

'Yes, he does. I love him, too.'

'Fergus or Angus?' Jacqui asked with a twinkle in her eyes.

Amy tried to look stern but it didn't quite work. 'I guess they both have their good points,' she finally conceded. 'But so far the dog's way out in front.'

Jacqui grinned delightedly. 'You're perfect for him. Just perfect.'

'My mother will have a coronary if I tell her I'm thinking about getting involved with a cop.'

'I bet your mother will change her mind as soon as she meets him. Why don't you ask her to come and visit you?'

Amy pointed to the mobile phone on her desk, her tone wry as she said, 'I just got a text from her. She's already on her way.'

CHAPTER THIRTEEN

'BUT darling,' Grace Tanner said as she looked around the tiny room at the hotel she had been assigned. 'This is just *ghastly*. Isn't there something better than this?'

'You can have mine if you like,' Amy offered. 'I think it's a tiny bit bigger than this one.'

'I can't believe you're putting up with this,' Grace said. 'Surely there's somewhere else you can stay.'

Amy decided against telling her mother of the alternative. 'It's fine, Mum. It's only for another ten weeks.'

Grace ran a finger over the top of the dresser and frowned at the dust that came off. 'Sweetie, I'm worried about you,' she said as she turned to face her. 'What if there are…?' She paused delicately over the word and then whispered, '*Spiders?*'

'I'm OK with spiders,' Amy assured her with

feigned confidence. 'I told you, I got completely desensitised in London.'

Grace folded her arms and gave her a motherly all-seeing look. 'You surely don't expect me to believe *that.*'

'All right,' Amy confessed with a little sigh, 'I'm not completely cured, but the only spider I've seen was handled very well…by someone…'

Grace's brows rose in speculation. 'So who was this someone? Someone…*special?*'

Amy took a deep breath and mentally prepared herself for the fall out. 'He's one of the local cops.'

'*A cop?*'

'I knew you'd say that.'

'Well, what else did you expect me to say?'

'He's not like Dad.'

'He's a cop, Amy,' Grace said, tightening her mouth. 'They're *all* like your father. They have issues.'

Amy rolled her eyes. 'Issues smissues. Well, guess what—doctors have *issues*. In fact, I bet even vets have issues.'

'Maybe, but their *issues* don't ruin people's lives,' Grace said. 'Come on, darling, surely you're not considering *a cop?*'

'You make it sound like some sort of nasty disease.'

'It is,' Grace said with conviction. 'You're doing the whole rewriting-the-past thing. I read about it in a magazine. It's a recipe for disaster. Women go looking for a chance to rewrite what went wrong in their lives and they end up marrying a version of their father.'

'I'm not going to *marry* the guy, Mum.'

Her mother gave her a probing look. 'But you're interested in him, aren't you?'

Amy blew out a frustrated breath. 'Is that a crime?'

'Bordering on one, yes, and it'll turn into one if you let it get out of hand. What's he offering?'

'A house with a spectacular view, a bathroom of my own, no spiders and *no* snoring next door.'

'*Snoring?*' Grace frowned. 'You mean someone *snores* next door?'

'The last reading was seven on the Richter scale.'

'Oh, my God,' Grace said. 'Maybe there are worse things than cops as boyfriends.'

'He's not my boyfriend,' Amy said. 'In fact, I wouldn't even go as far as saying we're friends.'

'So what's he got going for him?'

'He's got a beautiful dog,' Amy said. 'A German shepherd, and he loves me.'

'The dog or the cop?'

'The dog, of course!'

Grace tapped her bottom lip thoughtfully. 'I guess a quick fling would be all right.'

'I can't believe you said that!'

'It's been more than eighteen months since that wimpy Simon let you down,' Grace said. 'What you need is a bit of fun to set you right.'

'With a cop?'

'Yes, well, occasionally we have to scrape the bottom of the barrel, but as long as you don't promise him for ever, you should come out on top.'

'*Mu-um.*'

Grace gave her a guileless look. 'What?'

'I'm *not* going to go off and have fun with Angus Ford.'

'So that's his name, is it?'

'He's a control freak.'

'Has he booked you yet?'

'He came very close.'

'What stopped him?'

'I'm not sure,' Amy said.

'It was probably your legs,' Grace said, 'or your cleavage.'

'*Mu-um!*'

'If you've got it, flaunt it, darling. And you've definitely got it. At least you take after me in that regard and not your father.'

'Maybe Dad had some issues…you know, being a cop and all. It's not an easy job. They have to deal with such awful tragedy, their lives are in constant danger. I've been thinking about it a lot lately.'

This time it was Grace who rolled her eyes. 'If you're tuning up the violin, forget it. Your father was damaged when I met him and I stupidly thought I'd be the one to make a difference in his life. Some people are beyond help, darling. It's like some of the animals I treat. Some are too traumatised to recover. There's nothing you can do.'

'So you think Dad was like that?'

Grace let out a sigh as she reached for Amy's hands. 'Listen, sweetie. I loved your father. I loved him desperately, but he came with baggage. That baggage was like a third person in our relationship. I don't want you to go through what I went through. Go and find some boring accountant to fall in love with. Sleep with this guy if you want to get it out of your system, but in future stay away from cops. Believe me, they're not worth it.'

Amy bit her lip and confessed, 'But I think I'm falling in love with him.'

Grace threw her hands in the air. 'I knew it! I just knew it was a mistake, coming here, and so did your aunt and uncle. Lindsay did what she did and nothing anyone could do or say was going to stop her. I know you feel guilty about her life but that's the way it goes. She was who she was and you are who you are. You have to let it go, Amy. She was a suicide statistic waiting to happen. Coming here hasn't changed that, now, has it?'

'Yes, it has,' Amy said. 'I think there's more to her death than what we've been told.'

Grace frowned again. 'What are you saying?'

'She was happy here, Mum. You know she was. She was happy in a way she had rarely been before. And she didn't leave a note.'

'That doesn't mean anything, darling. When she tried to kill herself the other times she didn't leave a note either.'

'I know but I still feel uneasy…'

'What does this cop you're falling in love with think about your suspicions?'

'He's not happy about me contradicting his verdict, that's for sure.'

'What does he look like?'

'He's tall,' Amy said, lifting her hand as high above her head as she could get it. 'And he's got olive colouring and the most amazing brown eyes. They go almost black when he's angry.'

Grace's brows moved upwards. 'So you've got him angry already, have you?'

'Yes, well, we didn't exactly hit it off the first day.'

'So when can I meet him?'

'He's out of town at present,' Amy said. 'I'm not sure when he's due back.'

'Come on, then,' Grace said, picking up her handbag. 'Take me to the nearest café. I'm dying for a skinny soy decaf *lattè*.'

'Er…Mum…' Amy gave her mother an I-hate-to-be-the-one-to-tell-you-this grimace. 'There is no café in Marraburra.'

'*No café?*'

'There's a fish and chip shop but the coffee is

instant, the tea is dusty and I'm absolutely sure I haven't seen any soy milk anywhere in town.'

Grace let out a sigh of defeat. 'All right,' she said. 'Let's go downstairs to the pub and have a glass of something bubbly.' She gave her daughter a hopeful look and added, 'I don't suppose they have Bollinger or Moët?'

Amy shook her head. 'No but you can make up for it by drinking my share. I'm on call while the other doctor is away.'

'What! You mean you're running the medical clinic for the whole town on your own?' Grace said as she threaded her arm through her daughter's on the way down the stairs.

'That's about the situation at the moment, yes, but after a hectic start last week it's been pretty quiet since. I even had time to catch up on some journals.' Amy had barely finished speaking when her mobile phone rang.

'Sorry to call you after hours,' Teresa said. 'But I've got a young mother here with a three-year-old with a foreign object up his nose.'

'I'll be right there.' She hung up the phone and turned to her mother. 'Sorry, Mum, but something's come up, gone up actually, at the clinic. I shouldn't be any longer than ten or fifteen minutes.'

'Don't worry,' Grace said, and pushed open the door of the bar. 'I'll wait for you here. You never know.' She gave a little wink. 'I might even pick up a man for myself.'

'*Mu-um!*' Amy groaned.

She was halfway across the road to the clinic when she heard the screech of brakes and a cloud of dust rose in front of her as Angus brought his police vehicle to a halt on the side of the road.

'Oops,' she mouthed at him, wincing at his reproving frown and waggling finger.

He got out of the car and came to stand in front of her on the gravelled edge. 'Didn't your mother ever teach you to look both ways before crossing a street?' he asked.

'Er…funny you should mention my mother,' Amy said, pointing to the pub. 'She's in there right now, insisting on Bollinger. I hope Bill can handle her.'

'I'll go and introduce myself, or do you think I should get out of uniform first?'

Amy gave him a twisted smile. 'Take Fergus

with you,' she said. 'Then at least you're in with a chance.'

He grinned as she walked the few short steps to the clinic. 'See you around, Dr Tanner,' he called out after her.

She turned to look back at him, her cheeks a delicate shade of pink. 'See you, Sergeant Ford,' she answered, before disappearing inside.

'Hi, I'm Dr Tanner,' Amy introduced herself to an extremely thin, harried-looking young mother trying to control a hyperactive little boy with no success. The waiting room looked as if a whirlwind had recently passed through it, the few well-thumbed magazines now strewn over the floor interspersed with the collection of toys scattered from one end of the room to the other.

'Stop that, Nathan,' the mother growled, and wrenched her son up from the floor by one arm. 'Do you want a smack?'

The little boy gave his mother a pugnacious look and poked his tongue out. Amy watched in horror as the young woman walloped him with an open palm on his little legs, leaving a red handprint.

'Oh, please, don't do that,' Amy said, and came over to where the child was howling like a banshee.

'He's a brat,' Shontelle Kenton said with a scowl. 'I can't do nothing with him half the time. He's ruined my life. I wish he'd never been born.'

Amy did her best to disguise her shock at the woman's blunt statement, everything in her revolting at such harsh treatment towards a small child. But looking at the mother, she realised Shontelle was barely an adult herself—she couldn't have been more than eighteen, if that.

'Hi, Nathan,' she said, bending down to the hiccuping little boy. 'My name is Amy.'

'He won't talk,' Shontelle said. 'He hardly ever talks.'

Amy straightened and faced the sour-faced mother. 'I think it would be best if we take Nathan into the examination room and have a close look at his nose. Teresa said you'd seen him poke a plastic bead in his right nostril, right?'

'Yeah,' Shontelle said with a filthy look towards her son. 'He did it this morning and now it's runny and he's been sneezing. It's driving me nuts.'

'We'll give him a small dose of Phenergan to calm him down,' Amy explained. 'Once it takes effect I'll be able to inspect the nostrils and hope-fully retrieve the bead.'

Nathan took the medication without demur, happily distracted by Amy's stethoscope. After about fifteen minutes, chatting while they waited for the sedation to take affect, Amy found out Shontelle was a single mother, having been deserted by Nathan's father when she'd been just fifteen and pregnant.

'It must be hard for you, living out here,' Amy said as she inspected the child's right nostril with a nasal speculum and light. 'Do you have parents or family living nearby?'

'My dad owns a couple of fishing boats,' the girl said. 'He's away a bit, off the coast. My mother left when I was thirteen. Haven't seen her since.'

'Do you ever get a break from Nathan?' Amy asked as she located a green bead lodged a cen-timetre into the right nostril. 'Perhaps a female friend to mind him for you occasionally?'

The girl let out a sigh. 'I used to have a couple of friends but they've moved on now. I know this guy down at the boatyard, Josh. He some-times plays with Nathan but it's not regular.'

Amy sprayed the child's nostril with 4 per cent Xylocaine spray and then, gently inserting a wire loop behind the bead, she extracted it. 'There, all done,' she said, and smiled at the drowsy little boy, who sat blinking up at her with huge caramel-brown eyes.

'Can we go now?' Shontelle asked.

'Sure, but I'd like to see you both tomorrow in the clinic,' Amy said. 'Has Nathan had any routine checks done lately—height, hearing, weight?'

'I can't afford to go to the doctor all the time,' she said with another surly look.

'Who has been looking after you both up till now? Dr Peddington or Dr Ridley?'

'I saw Dr Peddington about a year ago when Nathan had an ear infection. I haven't been back since.'

Amy took them through to the reception area and made an appointment for the following afternoon. Writing it on a card, she handed it to the young mother. 'My mobile number is on that so if you are worried about Nathan, call me. It doesn't matter what time of day or night.'

'Thanks…' Shontelle gave her self-conscious look. 'I wasn't sure what to expect when I heard you were the mad lady's cousin. But you're nice. Real nice.'

'So you knew Lindsay?' Amy asked, trying not to feel too offended by the girl's comments in regard to her cousin.

'Not really. I saw her now and again when she came into town. She talked to herself a lot, which was a bit weird. But who wouldn't start talking to themselves around here? I feel like doing it myself when I'm stuck with a screaming kid all day.'

'Come and see me tomorrow. I'll check Nathan's nose again and have a look at his general health, and we'll have a chat about some parenting techniques that might help you handle him a little better,' Amy said. 'Don't be too hard on yourself, Shontelle. You've had a rough start to parenting, being so young and with so little support. You can turn it all around, it's not too late. Nathan is a sweet little boy who loves his mummy very much. He's just trying to get your attention because he feels a bit insecure right now.'

Tears shone in the young girl's eyes as she looked down at her little son. 'I don't really wish he hadn't been born,' she said, scrubbing at her face with the back of her hand. 'I just sometimes wish I had my mum around to help me, you know?'

Amy nodded as she patted the girl's thin shoulder. 'I understand, Shontelle. You're doing the best you can do, that's all that matters for now.'

'Do you really think I can change my life?' the girl asked as she clutched her little son's hand. 'You know…become a better mother?'

'Of course you can. You're not a bad person, Shontelle, and Nathan is not a bad child. You can come to me any time for help. I really mean that.'

Shontelle gave her a shaky smile. 'Thanks…'

Amy went back to the pub to find her mother sitting at a table, chatting with Angus.

Grace looked up and beamed at her proudly. 'You're not going to believe this, darling, but I've solved our little accommodation problem,' she said. 'We're moving in with Sergeant Ford right away. I've already packed our things. Isn't that kind of him to offer to give us two rooms rent-free?'

Amy lifted her brows as she met Angus's glinting dark brown gaze. 'I can see this matter has been taken out of my hands,' she said in a clipped tone. 'Rent-free, huh?'

'No strings, Dr Tanner,' Angus said with a hint of a smile. 'You can stay as long as you like.'

'I'm only going to be here for another couple of days,' Grace said to him. 'But Amy will be here for at least another ten weeks. Are you sure it's not going to put you out too much to have her under your feet for all that time?'

Amy glowered at her mother.

'Not at all,' Angus said as he got to his feet. 'I'll take the bags out to my car while you settle up with Bill.'

Amy waited until she and her mother were alone to give her a pointed look. 'So what happened to stay-away-from-cops-they're-nothing-but-trouble routine?' she asked.

Grace gave her a benign smile as she hoisted her handbag over her shoulder. 'Come on, darling, he's absolutely *gorgeous*. I can see why you fancy yourself in love with him. I'm halfway there myself and I've only just met him. Besides that, he's nothing like your father.'

Amy's expression was sceptical. 'You can tell that from one meeting?'

'He spoke of Lindsay with a great deal of respect,' Grace said. 'And he likes dogs. That's always a huge plus in a man.'

'I think you should know I have spent the best part of two weeks resisting his offer of accommodation,' Amy said. 'I've created enough gossip in this town without putting more fuel on the fire by moving in with him.'

Grace looped her arm through her daughter's. 'Don't worry, darling,' she said with an impish smile. 'I'll be the perfect chaperone. You just wait and see.'

CHAPTER FOURTEEN

'WHERE'S your mother?' Angus asked as he came into the kitchen the following morning.

'She took Fergus out for a walk,' Amy said. 'I hope you don't mind.'

He leant into the fridge to take out the orange juice. 'Why should I mind?'

Amy bit her lip before answering, 'She might be three hours.'

He turned to look at her. 'No kidding?'

'She's a fitness fanatic. Her idea of a walk in the park is to circumnavigate the entire continent.'

He smiled lopsidedly and asked, 'So how did you sleep last night?'

'I got at least seven hours straight,' she said. 'It was heaven.'

A small silence settled into the space between them.

Amy examined her hands for a moment before

meeting his eyes again, her gaze narrowing as she looked at his eyebrow. 'You've had the stitches removed,' she said.

His hand came up and traced the red line of his scar. 'Yeah, I did it myself.'

'I hope you used sterile instruments.'

'I did.'

The clock on the wall ticked the next few seconds…one… two…three…four…

'Angus…' She moistened her mouth and continued, 'I want to apologise for being so antagonistic towards you ever since I came to town.'

'It's fine,' he said. 'Your mother told me a little bit about your father. He sounds like a real charmer.'

'Yes, well, he certainly knew how to press the right buttons,' she said. 'But I realise now it was wrong to paint you with the same brush. I'm sorry.'

'Apology accepted.'

'Jacqui told me about your partner Daniel Fergusson.'

His expression tightened. 'I see.'

'She also told me about Carl's family, how you were the first on the scene. That must have been particularly harrowing so soon after the loss of your friend and colleague.'

'Yes, well, that's life in the force. You win some, you lose some.' He put his glass down on the bench as if it were a punctuation mark on the subject.

'Angus…'

'I've got to go,' he said. Sending her a keep-away look, he added, 'You're staying in this house as a guest, not a therapist. I would appreciate it if you would remember that in future.'

Amy opened her mouth to defend herself but he had already snatched up his keys and gone.

Amy went out to Reception after her last patient and looked over Helen's shoulder at the appointment book. 'Did Shontelle Kenton cancel her appointment with Nathan? I was expecting her an hour ago.'

'Her father called earlier,' Helen said. 'He said she'd changed her mind about coming to see you.'

Amy frowned. 'Her father called? Why didn't she cancel it herself?'

'Look, Amy, Barry Kenton's had a hard time with that girl,' Helen said. 'She's been a bit of a handful ever since her mother left. Barry does what he can to help her but she's a moody little miss. And that brat of hers is going to be trouble later on, if you ask me. He's virtually uncontrollable, as you saw yesterday.'

'He's just a little kid, Helen,' Amy protested. 'And she's only a kid herself. Besides, there's no such thing as a bad child, just a child in a bad place. Shontelle hasn't had the help she needs to cope with the demands of child care, but she could be taught.'

'You're wasting your time on that one,' Helen warned. 'Besides, why bother? You won't be here long enough to make a difference.'

'I don't believe that,' Amy said. 'The right person at the right time can make the most amazing difference in someone's life.'

'You should save your Girl Guide deed for the day for someone who will actually appreciate it,' Helen said as she pushed herself away from the desk. 'I'm off for the day. I hope things are quiet tonight for you. How's your mum settling in? I heard you've both bunked down with Angus, and about time, too.'

'Yes, well, I sort of got railroaded into it, but at least I slept well.'

'You'll need another good night's sleep because you've got a pretty full day tomorrow,' Helen said, pointing to the heavily pencilled appointment book. 'Even Carl Haines has booked in to see you.'

'Oh?'

'He'll just want a repeat prescription for his antidepressants and a cry on your shoulder, poor man.' She took her bag out of the bottom drawer of the desk and added, 'You know, I don't think he would still be with us if it hadn't been for Angus. Your cousin, too, when it comes down to it. Her death hit him pretty hard.'

Amy's brows came together. 'Carl was upset by Lindsay's death?'

Helen nodded. 'Lindsay painted some pictures of his wife and kids for him not long after the accident. She rode her rusty bike all the way out to take them to him. It touched him very deeply.'

Amy felt tears prickle at the back of her eyes. How like Lindsay to reach out to someone drowning in despair in spite of her own desperate struggle to keep on top of things.

'Well, I'd better get going,' Helen said. 'See you in the morning.'

'Yes… See you…' Amy said vaguely, as her eyes went to the desktop folder on the computer containing the list of patients' names and addresses. The Kentons lived a short distance from Marraburra Point and she quickly jotted down the address before locking up for the evening.

The road leading to the Kentons' house was smoothly tarred and landscaped on either side with flowering native plants. The house itself was large and modern and a shiny-top model BMW was parked in the open four-car garage. Amy couldn't help recalling the scruffy clothes and unkempt appearance of Shontelle when she had come to the clinic the day before. Amy had been expecting the girl's home to be a reflection of the same level of neglect, but nothing could have been further from the truth. She hadn't expected a fisherman to live so comfortably, but, then, Shontelle had said her father owned a couple of fishing boats. There were obviously a whole lot bigger than she'd realised.

A man in his early fifties came out as soon as she arrived, his face open and friendly as he came to greet her. 'Hello, I'm Barry Kenton.

You're Amy Tanner, the new locum, aren't you? I've heard all about you.'

Amy gave him her hand. 'Yes, I am. Nice to meet you, Mr Kenton.'

'What can I do for you, Dr Tanner? And, please, call me Barry.'

'Thank you, and my name is Amy,' she said, and then added, 'I was wondering if your daughter was home. She, or at least the receptionist, said you had cancelled her appointment this afternoon and I was worried about her. Is she here?'

A bleak look came over his features. 'I'm sorry, Amy. My daughter is totally unreliable, as you have no doubt noticed. She's gone off somewhere with my grandson, I don't know where. She's like that—a bit wild, if you know what I mean. I do what I can but she's a law unto herself.'

'I understand.'

Barry's expression looked pained. 'I wish I knew what to do. Ever since my wife left when Shoni was thirteen, things have gone downhill. I can't control her. I lie awake at night, worrying about little Nathan, but what can I do?'

Amy felt deeply for the man's distress. How many times had she heard the same story from other parents who, in spite of the loving upbringing they had given them, their child was hell-bent on rebellion?

'I wish I could say something to help you,' she said.

Barry moved his lips upwards into a loose version of a smile. 'I appreciate you coming out all this way to show your concern. I hear you're only here for three months. You're not thinking of extending your stay?'

'Not at this point,' she said.

There was an almost immeasurable silence.

'I'm so sorry about your cousin,' Barry said. 'She was a lovely lady. I had a lot of time for her.'

Amy was so used to concealing her surprise it came almost naturally this time. 'You knew her personally?'

'Yes,' he said. 'I often gave her a lift to town whenever I was going past. It's nice that you've come all this way to see where she lived. Were you very close to her?'

'No, not as much as I used to be,' she confessed. 'She... We grew apart over the years.'

'It's understandable,' he said. 'Drugs can do terrible things to people, can't they?'

Amy looked at him for a moment. 'She told you about her drug history?'

There was another infinitesimal pause before he answered. 'I've seen it before. It's a pathway to hell. But what can you do? I'm terrified my daughter might get into it, if she hasn't already.'

'I'll try and speak to Shontelle when I get the chance,' Amy offered. 'You never know, I might be able to help in some small way.'

Barry gave her a grateful smile. 'I'd really appreciate that. She's not been the same since my wife left. A girl needs her mother, especially when she becomes a mother herself. I've tried to be the best father I can, but it's never going to be enough.'

'None of us can do more than our best,' Amy said, and held out her hand. 'It was nice meeting you, Barry.'

'And you, Amy,' he said with a firm, friendly grasp. 'And thank you for your concern. It's greatly appreciated.'

What a pity there weren't more fathers like

that in the world, Amy thought as she drove away a few moments later.

'Where's my mother?' Amy asked when she encountered Angus in the kitchen on the return to his house.

'She's taken a bus trip up north to Monkey Mia,' he informed her. 'She left a note on the bench. She'll be back in two days' time.'

Amy frowned as he handed it to her. It was there in black and white…bright pink and white actually, she noticed with an inward smile. Unlike her father, her mother had never been a black-and-white person.

'What would you like for dinner?' Angus asked.

Amy put the note to one side. 'I don't expect you to cook me dinner.'

'I have to cook for myself so I may as well do enough for two,' he said. 'We can make up a roster if you like—that is, if you can cook.'

She sent him a withering glance from beneath her lashes. 'For your information, I happen to be a very good cook. My mother and I went to classes. We even went to Italy to a cookery school in Tuscany.'

'I'll look forward to seeing what you can do. How about we do alternate nights, unless one of us gets called out?'

'Fine.'

Amy watched as he began to slice some vegetables, his movements so deft and assured she couldn't help being impressed. Simon had barely been able to open a can, let alone prepare a meal from scratch.

'Carl Haines is coming in to see me tomorrow,' she said into the silence.

He looked up in between transferring the stir-fry vegetables to a bowl. 'He's not really an alcoholic,' he said. 'He's just a man who's had a bit too much tragedy to deal with at one time. He'll pull himself out of it eventually.'

'Helen told me Lindsay had done some paintings for him, of his wife and daughters.'

He resumed slicing carrots and shallots into slivers. 'It was a nice gesture. It showed she understood a bit of what he was going through.'

'It's hard what life dishes up sometimes,' Amy said as she fiddled with a stray strip of carrot skin and began curling it around her finger. 'People get up and go to work the same as usual and then in the blink of an eye everything changes. Their loved ones are snatched away from them. I don't think I'll ever get used to it, you know…death and dying.'

Angus put his knife down and looked at her. 'You have to toughen up or it will take you down,' he said. 'Especially in a place like this, where a lot of the people you treat are known to you personally.'

'How do you switch off?' she asked. 'I just can't do it.'

'You have to do it.'

'I'm not sure I want to stop feeling for people,' she said. 'I need to be able to feel for them so I can help them.'

'I'm not saying don't feel for them, but unless you develop some clinical distance you'll skew your judgement and end up doing more harm than good.'

'You sound like Helen,' she said. 'She told me I was wasting my time with Shontelle Kenton, but I can't help feeling that girl really needs a guiding hand.'

Angus's hands stilled on the wok he'd just taken from the cupboard. 'You've met her?'

'And her little boy. They came to the clinic late yesterday—he had a bead up his nose. I was going to see them when I…er…almost ran into you. Shontelle agreed to come back today to have a chat with me about parenting techniques, but she didn't turn up. Her father cancelled the appointment. I went out to their house before I came home.'

His eyes held hers. 'Did you meet Barry?'

'Yes,' she said. 'I thought he was lovely. He was terribly worried about his daughter and his grandson. He's worried Shontelle might be into drugs. He was quite open about it.'

'Did he mention his wife?'

'Only that she left when Shontelle was thirteen,' she said. 'It was funny, you know. After meeting Shontelle and Nathan in the clinic, I was expecting her to be living in a shabby council house, but the Kenton place is like a mansion. Barry's car is the latest model BMW. I didn't realise there was so much money in fishing.'

'Yes, well, there's fishing and there's fishing.'

Something about his tone brought Amy's eyes back to his. 'You think there's something shady about him?'

'Did I say that?'

'You didn't have to. I can see it in your eyes.'

'Look,' Angus said, deciding to be up front about it, 'I think you should stay well away from Barry Kenton and, yes, even his daughter. Your Mother Teresa mission is not going to get off the ground with people like that. Anyway, you'll be gone in a matter of weeks and they'll go back to what's familiar before you've driven past the Marraburra turn-off.'

'But what if I didn't leave when my time's up?' The words came out before she'd known she was going to say them. 'What if I decided to stay a little longer?'

His dark brown eyes pinned hers. 'How much longer are you talking about?'

'I don't know…six months, a year maybe.'

'I think you should leave as planned.'

Amy stared at him in affront. 'You don't think I'm doing a good job?'

'I don't think you belong here. Besides, you came here for all the wrong reasons.'

'Only according to you,' she threw back. 'You don't like me asking questions about my cousin, do you? You've made it clear right from the word go, but it makes me all the more determined to prove you wrong.'

'You're wasting your time.' His voice tightened in anger. 'Your cousin took her own life. Get over it.'

Amy got to her feet and, slamming her hand on the bench, glared at him. 'I will not get over it. I know there's something suspicious about her death and I also know you're trying to stop me from finding out what it is.'

'You're a doctor, not a detective,' he said. 'Stick to what you know. This is not the sort of place you can wander about voicing suspicions without some sort of backlash.'

'Is that what you're worried about, Sergeant Ford?' she asked. 'That there's going to be some sort of backlash you can't handle?'

'No,' he said, moving from behind the bench to take her by the upper arms and pull her towards him. 'This is what I'm worried about not being able to handle.' And his mouth swooped down and captured hers beneath the scorching heat of his.

CHAPTER FIFTEEN

THE thought of resisting Angus never once entered Amy's head. She returned his kiss with the same fiery fervour he was bestowing on her, his tongue diving into her moist warmth with electrifying expertise. Every nerve in her body vibrated with need and every pore of her skin opened to receive his touch. His hands moved over her with urgency, moulding her to him, leaving her in no doubt of his arousal.

His mouth left hers to devastate her senses even further by finding the tender curve of her breast his hands had uncovered. Her spine shuddered with the first warm glide of his palm over her fullness, her tight nipple prodding him. She whimpered in the back of her throat when his mouth closed over her breast, the rasp of his tongue and the teasing, tantalising scrape of his teeth making her writhe against him.

Her body was screaming for more of him, all of him. She wanted to feel him in every secret dewy place, anointing her with the essence of his being, making her feel like a woman in the most timeless way of all.

It was a hit-and-miss scramble to his bedroom but Amy hardly noticed. Furniture toppled over in their wake, and Fergus yelped and backed away at one point as Angus misjudged the distance from the hall to the bedroom door.

They landed in a tangle of limbs on his bed, the mattress springing with their weight, bringing her into closer contact with the rigid heat of his body.

Clothes went in all directions, and for the first time Amy gave no thought to the consequences of sleeping with a man just for the sheer irresistible force of out-of-control desire that was storming through her being like a tumultuous tide.

She vaguely registered the tearing sound of a condom being unwrapped from its tiny package, and then her senses soared when Angus's hard strong body entered hers in a smooth but spine-arching movement that left her totally breathless.

Her climb to paradise was faster than any she'd ever experienced. It was as if every cell of her body had been preparing for this moment for years and now it was heading towards a cataclysmic release that had no equal.

She felt herself lift off as he drove harder, as if he too was chasing an exhilarating release that had so far escaped him. Her body tightened around him, her panting breaths rising in tempo as she reached the pinnacle of pleasure. A thousand lights exploded in her head, the tiny cascading particles dancing around the perimeter of her consciousness as she felt his final plunge into oblivion…

Amy must have briefly drifted off as she woke to the sensation of one of his hands stroking up and down her arm. She turned and looked at him, her fingers going up to his mouth, tracing its contours. He captured her finger with his mouth and sucked on it, his eyes holding hers.

She gave a little giggle and tried to pull her finger out. 'Let go.'

'No,' he said, holding her with his teeth.

'Are you taking me as your prisoner, Sergeant Ford?' she asked, her stomach kicking in excitement when he rolled her under him again.

'Damn right I am,' he growled, and took her on

another fast and furious ride to fulfilment, leaving her boneless and weak in his arms.

Amy had never been good at this part, the moment after the madness. Even with Simon she had felt awkward and self-conscious. She lay very still, breathing in the clean male scent of Angus as he lay relaxed over her, his face buried in the soft skin of her neck, the whisper of his breath like a teasing feather against her.

Angus lifted himself off and looked down at her. 'I don't know about you, but I never really know what to say at times like this.'

'I guess, thanks for the memories sounds a bit tacky, huh?'

His brows moved together slightly. 'Yeah, it does.'

'How about let's enjoy this while it lasts?' she said after a tiny pause. 'I mean, that's all you're offering, isn't it? A short-term fling?'

His expression clouded even further as he looked down at her mouth. 'I'm not sure what I'm offering,' he said. 'Up until a few moments ago I would have said we had nothing in common and that the sooner you left town the better, but now I'm not so sure.'

She gave him a twisted look. 'What are you saying, Sergeant Ford, that you might want me to stay around a bit longer after all?'

His dark brown eyes glinted as they homed in on hers. 'I'm not sure what I'm saying but I certainly know what I'm feeling right now.'

Amy could feel it too…

She woke to the sound and feel of her stomach growling with hunger. She pushed herself up on her elbows to find Angus standing by the bedside, watching her.

'I've made dinner. Are you hungry?' he asked.

She brushed her wild hair out of her eyes. 'I'm starving.'

He held out a hand and she slipped hers into it, his strength as he pulled her upright thrilling her as her naked body brushed against the hard frame of his. He lowered his mouth to hers, kissing her lingeringly, the taste of his lips and tongue sending her into a maelstrom of feeling.

He pulled away to look down at her, his hands still cupping the sides of her face. 'I think I should tell you that this sort of thing didn't happen with my previous boarder.'

She smiled at his dry tone. 'I'm assuming the engineer from Broome wasn't female, then?'

'No, definitely not.' He stroked his thumbs along the curve of her cheeks for a moment as his eyes held hers.

'Angus?'

His thumbs stopped. 'Yes?'

Amy took a shaky breath. 'I think I should tell you that this sort of thing has never happened to me before.'

'You mean falling into bed with your landlord?'

'No, I mean falling in love with a man I only met a couple of weeks ago.'

There was a moment or two of air-tightening silence.

'"Love" is a very strong word,' he said. 'Aren't you confusing it with physical attraction?'

'I'm not sure…' She sank her teeth into her bottom lip, releasing it after a second to add, 'I never felt anything like this with my ex-fiancé. I didn't respond to him like I do to you, not ever. I feel something so powerful and electric every time you touch me. Do you feel it, too?'

'Amy.' He let out a sigh that sounded rough around the edges. 'I'm not sure I can promise you anything other than here and now. I've already gone down the permanent track and it didn't work out. My fiancé wasn't prepared to live the life I've been called to live. I know this probably sounds a bit crazy, but I didn't choose to be cop, not in the way others do. And, no, it has nothing to do with my father being a cop and his father before him. It was about me. My world view, my convictions, my need to contribute to the community in such a way as to make a difference.'

'But I feel like that, too!' she said. 'That's why I'm a doctor. I love helping people and making a difference.'

'I realise that, Amy, but my job requires certain sacrifices, gut-wrenching sacrifices that most women find hard to cope with.' He released her to rake a hand through his hair. 'When Dan died, I saw what it did to his wife. She lost her entire world, her purpose for living. She's still not on track. Her kids are traumatised, and will be for the rest of their lives. How could I do that to someone I cared about? It might not appear to be so out here, but sometimes my job is extremely dangerous. I've already had several death threats and I have no reason to believe they weren't serious.'

'Is that why you're here at Marraburra?' she asked.

It was a moment or two before he answered, and even when he did, Amy wondered if he was being straight with her. His expression had that keep-away look to it again, and it hurt her to have felt so close to him physically but so far away emotionally.

'I'm here to get a job done, simple as that.'

'And after that job is done?' she asked.

'I have a few options open to me,' he said. 'But I'm not prepared to discuss them right now.' He handed her a bathrobe with a small smile that should have softened the blow of his words but somehow didn't. 'You'd better put this on, otherwise I might forget that I've got dinner simmering on the cook-top.'

Amy slipped into the soft folds of the robe and tied the cord around her waist, her heart feeling as if it had been squeezed inside her chest as she asked, 'So what you're saying is we only have this time together?'

Angus lifted her chin to look into her dark blue eyes, the tug of temptation so strong he had to call on every gram of resistance to counteract it. 'Better to spend three months with someone you like than thirty years with someone you hate, right?'

'Ten weeks,' she said flatly. 'That's all we've got…'

He took the cord of her bathrobe and untied it, letting the garment drop to the floor at her feet. 'Then let's not waste a minute of them,' he said, and pulled her back into his arms.

Amy had just finished treating a woman with biliary colic the next day and organised a gall-bladder ultrasound for her to Geraldton when Helen informed her that Carl Haines had can-celled his appointment.

'Did he give a reason?' Amy asked as she handed the receptionist the last patient's notes to be filed.

'He said he's too sick to drive into town,' Helen said. 'But that could mean he's been drinking and didn't want to risk being pulled over by Angus or one of the other cops.'

'I'll go and visit him at home,' Amy said. 'What's his address?'

Helen gave it to her on a piece of paper. 'He

lives on a pretty rough road. I hope your car won't get a stone chip.'

'It doesn't matter,' Amy said as she pulled out her keys. 'I'm thinking of selling it anyway. It's totally unsuitable for out here.'

Helen's brows lifted. 'So are you thinking of staying longer?'

Amy gave her an inscrutable look as she swept past. 'I haven't quite made up my mind.'

Carl was sitting on the front verandah of his house when Amy pulled up, his bloodshot eyes narrowing as she came towards him.

'Hello, Carl, I thought since you weren't feeling well enough to come to see me, I'd come and see you,' she said.

'You shouldn't have bothered,' he said, looking away. 'I don't really care if I live or die anyway, so what need do I have of a doctor?'

Amy sat on the edge of the verandah next to him. 'You might not need a doctor but surely you could do with a friend?'

He turned his head to look at her, his expression so racked with pain she had trouble containing her emotions. Lines of grief roadmapped his face; his eyes were like murky hazel pools of bottomless grief and his skin had a sallow look to it as if it had grown tired of containing the sadness he was carrying in his body.

'I miss them so much…' He spoke after a long aching silence.

She touched his hand with one of hers. 'I know you do, Carl. You'll always miss them.'

'I want to get myself together but I can't face the years ahead without numbing the pain.' He gave a grunt of humourless laughter and continued, 'Funny thing is I wasn't even a drinker before I lost my wife and daughters. I had the occasional beer but I never really got into it in a big way, not like some of the other guys around here.'

'Bill told me you were on an antidepressant,' she said. 'Are you taking it regularly?'

'Not really… I guess I should, right?'

'Might be better than the drink,' she said. 'You really shouldn't be having both.'

'I know. Angus said the same.'

'He's a good friend to you, isn't he?'

'Yeah…' He gave her a little smile. 'So, are you his girlfriend now? I heard you moved in with him.'

'Just because I share his house doesn't necessarily mean I will be sharing his bed,' she said, hoping the colour of her cheeks weren't giving her away. *Or not for long anyway.*

Carl looked down at his dusty workboots for a moment. 'I'm glad you came out here to see me,' he said without looking at her. 'I have something to show you, you being Lindsay Redgrove's cousin and all.'

'I heard she was friendly with you.'

'She was,' he said. 'She gave me paintings and stuff. She even gave me one the day before she died.'

Amy blinked at him. 'Have you still got it?'

'Course I have,' he said. 'I just wish I'd been here when she dropped it off… I might have been able to talk to her, you know, to stop her doing what she did.'

'Can I see it?'

He got to his feet and beckoned for her to come inside. Amy stepped over the threshold and her eyes went immediately to the three portraits on the wall. Her cousin had never done anything so beautiful. The face of Carl's wife Julie showed warmth and love and a sparkling personality, and the two little girls had doll-like features and bright blonde curls, their engaging smiles bringing tears to Amy's eyes.

She vaguely registered the sound of Carl opening a cupboard and the crackle of a canvas being unrolled. She turned as he handed it to her.

'I'm not much of an abstract art lover myself,' he said. 'The portraits she did of Julie and Katie and Meg were the only realistic things she did, so I don't really know what this is meant to represent. But I kept it because she left it on the doorstep, I guess as a sort of goodbye.'

Amy looked down at the painting in her hands and felt a shiver of something indefinable pass over her skin. The painting was as Carl said, abstract, but even with the crude slashes and strokes of the brush she could make out the figure of a woman on a beach, running away from what looked like hundreds of rectangular white shells.

Amy swallowed and, lowering the painting, looked at Carl. 'Have you shown anyone this? The police, for instance?'

He shook his head. 'No. I didn't even think of it until someone said you were her cousin the other day. I just thought you might like to have something of hers to keep.'

'I would love to keep it, if you're sure you don't mind?'

He gave her another sad little smile. 'Why would I want that when I have these three?' he said, and pointed to his family on the wall.

Amy squeezed his hand and fought back tears. 'Thank you, Carl,' she said. 'You don't know how much this means to me or to Lindsay.'

Amy was on her way back to Angus's place when she received a call from Barry Kenton, who informed her Shontelle and Nathan were now at home if she wanted to drop by and check on the little boy's nose.

'I offered to drive Shoni and the boy into the clinic to see you, but she refused,' he said with a frustrated sigh. 'I thought if you just dropped around casually, it might be easier. I hope you don't mind. I know you're probably busy and it is the end of the day but I thought it was too good an opportunity to miss.'

'Not at all, Barry,' she said. 'I'm only a few minutes away. I've just finished a house call nearby.'

'And here I was thinking doctors didn't do house calls any more,' he said. 'See you soon.'

'Where's Dr Tanner?' Angus asked Helen as he came into the clinic with quick urgent strides.

'She's on a house call to Carl,' Helen answered. 'Have you tried her phone?'

'It keeps going to the message bank,' he said, trying to stem the panic flooding his system. 'It must be turned off or out of range. I'll give Carl a call to see if she's still there.'

'What's wrong, Angus?' Helen asked. 'I've never seen you so on edge before. Is it something to do with Amy?'

'I can't talk right now,' he said as his fingers pressed the rapid dial on his phone. 'But if you see her, don't let her out of your sight and, whatever you do, don't let Barry Kenton anywhere near her.'

'B-Barry?' Helen put a hand up to her throat. 'Oh, dear… He called not two minutes ago, asking for Amy to call in at his place to see Shontelle and Nathan. I told him to call her on her mobile…'

Angus let out an expletive and flew out the door.

CHAPTER SIXTEEN

THE Kenton residence looked deserted when Amy first drove in but almost as soon as she had got out of the car the front door opened and Barry appeared with a welcoming smile on his face.

'Amy, I don't know how to thank you for taking such a special interest in my daughter and grandson.'

'Hi, Barry,' she said, taking his outstretched hand. 'It's my pleasure, really. I'm glad you called as I've been a bit worried about Nathan's nose. I want to make sure it hadn't become infected.'

'Come inside and make yourself comfortable and I'll call them both,' he said, leading her into the luxurious lounge area overlooking the ocean.

Amy turned to look at the view cast in an orange glow from the setting sun. She heard Barry call his daughter's name but as far as she could tell there was no answer. He came back into the room a short time later with an apologetic look on his face.

'I'm sorry about this, Amy, but I can't seem to find her anywhere. She's not answering.'

'Could she have slipped out without you noticing?' Amy asked. 'She drives, doesn't she?'

'Her car is in the garage,' he said, scratching his head.

'Maybe I should come back later.' She reached for her bag but he put his hand over hers and the bag fell back to the floor with a little thud.

'No,' he said with another smile as he stepped back. 'Please, don't leave just yet. I'm sure she's just taken Nathan for a little walk. Why don't we sit and have a drink until she returns?'

Amy would have refused except it had been hours since she'd had anything to drink and the thought of a tall glass of iced water was just too tempting to resist. 'All right,' she said, returning his smile.

Before she could stop him he bent down and picked up her bag. 'I'll put it on the bar over here,' he said. 'Nathan was eating a biscuit in here the other day and we've had ants ever since. I wouldn't want them to get in your bag.'

Amy inspected the floor at her feet as he took her bag away. Ants were OK as long as there were no spiders. She gave a little shiver and turned to face him again.

He held up a bottle of red wine and two glasses. 'How about a smooth red to finish the day?'

'I'm the only doctor in town at the moment so I'd better stick to water or something soft,' she said.

'Surely one little glass won't hurt?'

She shook her head. 'Sorry, Barry, but you go ahead. I'll be happy with a soda water.'

She watched as he opened a bottle of fizzy water and poured it into a glass, the chink of ice falling into the liquid suddenly sounding loud in the silence.

'You have a lovely home,' she said. 'Have you lived here long?'

'Ever since Shoni was a toddler,' he said. 'My wife and I moved here from the Northern Territory.'

'Shontelle told me you're a fisherman,' she said once they had sat down with their drinks. 'Are you away a lot?'

'Not as much as I used to be,' he said, taking a sip from a full glass of red wine. 'I'm at a time of life when I want to sit back and relax a bit, enjoy the benefits of all the hard work I've put in over the years.'

'I guess it must be quite a tough life, going out for a week at a time, leaving family and loved ones behind.'

'Yes.' He stared into the contents of his glass for a moment. 'That's why my wife left. She couldn't handle the loneliness.' He lifted his eyes back to hers and smiled. 'But that's old history. Tell me about you. How are you enjoying your stay in Marraburra? Have you settled your concerns over your cousin's suicide?'

Amy gave him a self-conscious look. 'So you've heard about my real reason for being here.'

'It's hard to keep a secret in a place the size of this,' he said with another smile. 'I heard you were interested in the details of your cousin's death.'

'Yes, so I decided to come here and do a little background research for myself.'

'And what have you found?' he asked.

Amy put her glass down and met his interested gaze. 'I don't actually think my cousin committed suicide.'

He held her gaze without blinking. 'You think she was murdered?'

'It's got to be one or the other, hasn't it? For one thing, she didn't leave a note…' She let the sentence fall away as she thought about the painting in her car.

Barry's brows rose slightly. 'Do you have any evidence to suggest foul play?'

'Not really,' she answered, 'although Carl Haines gave me a painting earlier today that made me wonder…'

'A painting?' His tone sharpened a fraction. 'A painting of what?'

Amy had hoped to speak to Angus before anyone else about Lindsay's canvas but she couldn't see any harm in telling Barry who, as a local, would surely be well aware of the drug problems along the coast.

'Lindsay left a painting on Carl's doorstep the day before she died. I might be wrong about this but I think she may have seen something suspicious along the beach—you know, drugs being dropped off or something.'

'Where is this painting at the moment?' he asked.

'It's in my car.'

'Can I have a look at it?' he asked. 'I might be able to help you solve your little mystery.'

Amy put her glass to one side and, picking up her keys, left him to go to her car, returning a few moments later with the canvas and rolling it out for him to look at.

He looked at it for a long time, the silence stretching and stretching until he broke it by saying, 'I think you're wrong, Dr Tanner.'

'What do you mean?'

He met her eyes with the ice blue of his own. 'Your cousin *did* commit suicide. There's never been any doubt of that. You have only to ask the police who investigated the circumstances of her death.'

'But this painting seems to suggest—'

His eyes hardened as he interrupted her. 'Your cousin had a drug problem since she was a teenager. This painting is just about what was going on in her head.'

'I don't agree,' Amy argued. 'Lindsay did have a drug history but she never touched a thing after she went to hospital. She was terrified of having another relapse into psychosis—the thought of being institutionalised again petrified her. I've heard along the Western Australian coast there are drop-off points for South-East Asian drugs. Boats go out to meet container ships and the drugs are offloaded, and some of the drug packages can go astray. What if Lindsay found some packages on the beach where she lived? It would be her worst nightmare that the one thing she'd travelled so far to avoid landed virtually on her doorstep.'

'That's an interesting theory, Amy. Maybe you should raise it with the police?' he said. 'It sounds a bit fanciful to me. I've never seen any drug drop-offs along this part of the coast.'

'I guess you wouldn't have, would you Barry?' Angus's voice spoke from the doorway.

'Sergeant Ford.' Barry was all politeness as he got to his feet. 'Would you care to join us in a drink?'

Amy felt the tension in the air as if someone had charged it with high-voltage electricity. She looked from one man to the other, her mind distantly assembling comments, thoughts and vague observations that hadn't fitted together before. Barry had said Shontelle's car was in the garage but when Amy had gone to get the painting only

Barry's black BMW had been there. Why had he lied about something like that?

Now there was no sign of the urbane host of earlier. He was like a cornered dog eyeing up an opponent, his body tense, hands opening and closing as if preparing to do battle.

'It's over, Barry,' Angus said.

'Over? What's over, Angus? I'm not following you,' Barry said, still with that cool polite smile in place.

'Your fishing business is over. Except it's not fish you've been hauling in, is it, Barry?'

'I'm really not with you, Sergeant,' Barry replied, moving to a closed cupboard next to the bar. 'We haul in our quota off the coast, nothing more—you can check the log.'

'Step away from the cupboard, Barry. The coastguard has already intercepted your latest catch. You've got your quota all right—pure heroin. Your men are all being charged by the drug squad down at the docks as we speak.'

'You're lying!' Barry threw back, all attempts to remain polite fading. 'You've got nothing on me. I've been here all along. I've got nothing to do with what those creeps have on those boats.'

'Haven't I?' Angus asked with a chilling smile. 'I have your daughter and grandson in protective custody. Josh Brumby brought her and Nathan in earlier today. She'd gone to him for help. She told me less than an hour ago how she overheard a phone conversation between you and one of your men about the guy you pushed over the cliff at Caveside Cove. Brent Handley was the hit man you engaged to murder your wife. He woke a couple of hours ago from his coma. Your wife didn't run away as you led everyone, including your own daughter, to believe, did she, Barry? You had her killed in cold blood because she wanted out of your operation. She threatened to spill the beans.'

Barry opened and closed his fists again, and backed away from the bar. Amy could tell he knew he was beaten. Angus had his gun trained on him and James and Tim Greenaway, the other junior constable, had already silently entered the room with guns at the ready.

'Dr Tanner was partially right, wasn't she, Barry?' Angus continued. 'Lindsay Redgrove probably would not have taken her own life except you put pressure on her when she found those packs of heroin on the beach after the last drop-off six months ago. Brent Handley didn't appreciate his assisted flight over the cliff—he's given a full account of your operation. He said you got him to threaten Lindsay. You knew it wouldn't take much to tip her over the edge. She killed herself the next day, frightened out of her mind that she would be institutionalised again if the drugs were somehow connected to her.'

Barry's mouth thinned into a hard tight line. 'You're making all this up to force a confession out of me. I'm not saying a thing until I speak to my lawyer.'

'We don't need a confession, Barry,' Angus said. 'Your daughter has told us everything we need to know. You've been controlling her with your fists for years. And you've been doing the same to her son. That's why you lured Dr Tanner here this evening, wasn't it? You couldn't find Shontelle and Nathan and it got you worried. You didn't like the fact that your daughter trusted the new doctor in town—couldn't have her blubbering to her, could you? I guess Dr Tanner not being convinced of her cousin's suicide must have topped it off for you, eh? That was just too risky, wasn't it, Barry? You had to do something and do it tonight.'

Barry sent a filthy glance towards Amy as the two other officers clipped handcuffs on him. 'You just had to come up here poking your nose around, didn't you? Well, you won't get away with this, I swear to God.'

'Make all the threats you like, Barry,' Angus said as he directed his men to take him out to the police van. 'But if ever you want to get to Dr Tanner, you'll have to deal with me first, because I won't be letting her out of my sight.'

Amy would have given anything to have had a chance to speak to Angus right then and there about that heart-stopping statement, but apart from a few parting words about how she was feeling, and her getting back home, the formal arrest and transfer of Barry Kenton, together with the rest of the drug squad operation, necessitated her having to wait.

She filled in the time checking her phone for missed calls. She hadn't realised that Barry had turned off her phone when he had taken her bag to the bar. There were ten missed calls from Angus and three from her mother. She listened to the messages, her heart swelling with hope when she heard the frantic tone of Angus's voice recorded there. She decided she was never going to erase them.

'Angus?' She came up at him at as the others were finally leaving.

He pressed a fingertip to her lips. 'Later,' he said. 'We have a lot to talk about but not here and not now. This is the middle of the biggest drug bust on the West Australian coast, not the place I want to ask you the most important question of all.'

Amy's jaw dropped open. *'You...you...mean...?'*

He winked at her as he opened her car door for her. 'Drive safely, Dr Tanner, and keep under the speed limit, OK?'

CHAPTER SEVENTEEN

AMY looked up at Angus a couple of hours later in amazement. 'Did you really mean it when you said you'd never be letting me out of your sight?'

He smiled as he pulled her closer. 'Of course I meant it. How else am I going to ensure you keep out of trouble unless I put you under permanent police guard?' He tapped her on the end of her up-tilted nose and added, 'You came speeding into town and very nearly undid two years of police work with all those questions about your cousin's death. I was so close to cracking the case, just waiting for the next big drop-off. We thought Barry might take the operation elsewhere because of the sudden interest you had in your cousin's suicide. He's been under close surveillance, but we've never had the proof. We called him the Chess Player—always a few moves ahead—a very smooth operator, as you found out for yourself.'

Amy winced in embarrassment. 'I'd practically nominated him for father of the year, he seemed so convincing about his worries over Shontelle and Nathan.'

'He's been more like the father from hell. It's probably why Shontelle got pregnant in the first place in a desperate attempt to get away, but it backfired when the father of her baby deserted her. We're investigating whether Barry had something to do with that, too—the father's vanished at this point. Maybe he got a little too close to stumbling onto Barry's operation.'

'What will happen to Shontelle and Nathan now?'

'I've already organised a police social worker to meet with her. If support can be arranged, she might be able to complete her high-school education and make something of her life for Nathan's sake. She has you to thank for that, you know. She now realises the cycle of violence could stop if she makes the right choices.'

'I'm glad I was able to help, even if I did nearly jeopardise your investigation in the process.'

'We both got the answers we were after,' he said. 'You found out the truth behind Lindsay's suicide and I closed down one of the biggest heroin suppliers in the country.' He pulled her closer, his voice deepening with emotion. 'I nearly went out of my mind when you didn't answer your phone. I realised then how much I loved you. I know I said I wasn't interested in anything long term, but nearly losing you made me have a rethink, which leaves me with just one other question I want an answer to.'

'Oh,' she said, smiling up at him rapturously. 'What question would that be?'

'Amy Tanner, will you spend the rest of your life by my side, to be my love, my companion, my strength and my purpose for living, no matter where our careers take us?'

Amy's eyes started to sparkle. 'Is that a proposal, Sergeant Ford?'

'It is indeed, Dr Tanner,' he said with a sexy smile. 'And is the doctor I love more than life itself by any chance saying yes?'

'Well, *of course* she is,' Grace said as she came into the room with her overnight luggage in one hand, a beaming smile splitting her face. 'Aren't you, darling?'

Amy rolled her eyes and groaned. *'Mu-um!'*

MEDICAL™

Large Print

Titles for the next six months...

March

THE SINGLE DAD'S MARRIAGE WISH — Carol Marinelli
THE PLAYBOY DOCTOR'S PROPOSAL — Alison Roberts
THE CONSULTANT'S SURPRISE CHILD — Joanna Neil
DR FERRERO'S BABY SECRET — Jennifer Taylor
THEIR VERY SPECIAL CHILD — Dianne Drake
THE SURGEON'S RUNAWAY BRIDE — Olivia Gates

April

THE ITALIAN COUNT'S BABY — Amy Andrews
THE NURSE HE'S BEEN WAITING FOR — Meredith Webber
HIS LONG-AWAITED BRIDE — Jessica Matthews
A WOMAN TO BELONG TO — Fiona Lowe
WEDDING AT PELICAN BEACH — Emily Forbes
DR CAMPBELL'S SECRET SON — Anne Fraser

May

THE MAGIC OF CHRISTMAS — Sarah Morgan
THEIR LOST-AND-FOUND FAMILY — Marion Lennox
CHRISTMAS BRIDE-TO-BE — Alison Roberts
HIS CHRISTMAS PROPOSAL — Lucy Clark
BABY: FOUND AT CHRISTMAS — Laura Iding
THE DOCTOR'S PREGNANCY BOMBSHELL — Janice Lynn

MILLS & BOON®
Pure reading pleasure